"I can test these smoke detectors for you, but I don't think that will really solve your problem."

"Why?"

"Because it's not really smoke you're afraid of." He pulled a book of matches out of his pocket and Jeannie fought the urge to flinch.

"You said you didn't need matches to test the smoke detectors," she reminded him.

"I don't," Chad said gently, "but you need them to test yourself. Jeannie, you need to get over this. You need to light a match."

"Oh, no, I don't!" Jeannie blurted out her refusal, even though she was embarrassed Chad had guessed her fear of flame. Did he have to strike such a nerve?

"Don't feel bad—I've seen sillier reactions on much more serious people. I can help. And I won't tell anyone."

Why would Chad Owens do something like this for her? Jeannie couldn't bring herself to ask the question.

Books by Allie Pleiter

Love Inspired

My So-Called Love Life
The Perfect Blend
*Bluegrass Hero
*Bluegrass Courtship
*Bluegrass Blessings
*Bluegrass Christmas
Easter Promises
  *"Bluegrass Easter"
Falling for the Fireman

*Kentucky Corners

Love Inspired Single Title

Bad Heiress Day
Queen Esther & the
  Second Graders of Doom

Love Inspired Historical

Masked by Moonlight
Mission of Hope
Yukon Wedding

ALLIE PLEITER

Enthusiastic but slightly untidy mother of two and RITA® Award finalist Allie Pleiter writes both fiction and nonfiction. An avid knitter and unreformed chocoholic, she spends her days writing books, drinking coffee and finding new ways to avoid housework. Allie grew up in Connecticut, holds a B.S. in speech from Northwestern University and spent fifteen years in the field of professional fundraising. She lives with her husband, children and a Havanese dog named Bella in the suburbs of Chicago, Illinois.

Falling for the Fireman
Allie Pleiter

Love Inspired

Recycling programs
for this product may
not exist in your area.

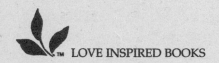

™ LOVE INSPIRED BOOKS

ISBN-13: 978-0-373-81604-0

FALLING FOR THE FIREMAN

www.LoveInspiredBooks.com

Printed in U.S.A.

Know also that wisdom is like honey for you:
If you find it, there is a future hope for you,
and your hope will not be cut off.
—*Proverbs* 24:14

Dedication

To first responders everywhere—
God bless your courage and dedication

Acknowledgments

Astute travelers will recognize Gordon Falls bears a striking resemblance to Galena, Illinois (the beautiful fire house and floodgates are dead giveaways). Jeannie and Chad's community owes all of its charm—and none of its faults—to the lovely town that inspired their story. Thanks to Don Lay, fire marshal of Carol Stream, Illinois; and to Mike Simmons, chief of the Galena, Illinois, fire department for their input and endurance of my endless questions. Any missed professional details are surely my own fault, and not related to their fine assistance. Special thanks to the Pokorn family for lending me their home while I "researched" peaceful atmosphere, great views, good food and awesome shopping. It is the people and places that make my job as wonderful as it is, and I'm forever grateful.

Chapter One

Gordon Falls, Illinois
September 2009

Jeannie Nelworth had the faucet handle in a death grip. It wasn't that the women's restroom of The Stew Pot restaurant was a tense place; she just hadn't expected her nerve to go out from under her quite so completely tonight. Somewhere between picking up name tags and the Merchant Association's first agenda item, she'd had to bolt into the ladies' room to pull herself together. She'd found the bright red wallpaper amusing before, but now it felt loud and suffocating.

Abby Reed was predictably right behind her. A best friend can usually see through faked calm, and Abby was as intuitive as they come.

"I'm okay," Jeannie lied the moment Abby pushed into the tiny room.

"You are *not* okay." Abby turned and threw the door's small dead bolt Jeannie had forgotten to latch. "I *told* Mary Hunnington not to ask you about postponing tonight's presentation, that you'd say 'go ahead' when you shouldn't have."

"I like being at these dinners." Jeannie forced a cheery tone, pulling her hand off the fixture to fuss with her long brown hair that didn't need fussing. It was true. Normally she did enjoy the monthly gathering of businesspeople in town. The many shopkeepers, hotel owners and restauranteurs that made up Gordon Falls were her family. Even the tourists were part of her life here. That's why it was so hard to have her sweetshop closed—if only for a while.

"Besides," she continued, "Nicky'd never forgive me for ruining his monthly videogame sleepover. Much as it kills me, that eighth-grade tornado loves a night away from his mom."

Abby sighed and gave her the look half the other merchants had. She knew her colleagues cared for her, only now their warm but pitying looks made her feel simultaneously welcome and on display. "Really, there isn't a soul here who would have blamed you if you missed this one. You're the *last* person who needs to hear tips on holiday lighting and fire safety."

Why bother waiting? Another thirty days wouldn't change the fact that her candy store and home had burned down a few weeks ago. "If I stayed home, what would that solve?" To stay home was admitting defeat, and Jeannie liked to think of herself as the kind of woman who gave no quarter to tragedies like that. "Okay, it's hard," she admitted, but even those three words felt too big, "but God is bigger than a burned building."

"It's not just a building, it was your home. And the home you had with Nicky. The home you had with Henry, God rest his soul. God is big, but that's *huge*."

Just the mention of her late husband's name was enough to double the size of the knot in her throat, even after half a dozen years. She'd loved her quaint shop down by the riverfront. It hadn't been close to the center of town, but she'd always thought that made it feel homey. It had been close enough to catch the riverfront tourists, and back then she, Henry and Nicky used to watch the sun come up over the river as they ate breakfast in their home above the shop.

Then Henry was gone. Now, six years later, the building was gone. "What's the whole point of faith if not to sustain me through something like this?"

Abby started in, but Jeannie just blinked back tears and shot her hand up in a silent "Don't."

After a quiet moment, Abby pulled a paper towel from the ancient metal dispenser and blotted her own tears. "George wants to talk to you," she said softly. A conversation with George Bradens, Gordon Falls's Fire Chief, usually meant getting roped onto a committee for some new civic endeavor. "He says it's about Nicky." Abby put a hand on Jeannie's shoulder. "Listen, this is too much. Let me make some excuse for you so you can go home."

"I'm fine."

Abby leaned against the red Formica countertop. "I thought we covered this already."

The room was far too red. Red tile, red wallpaper. It all felt like sirens going off, close and loud. "Well, I'm *close* to fine." That's how she chose to view the raw-around-the-edges feeling that had continued to plague her every day—every hour—since the fire. The entire month felt like peeling off singed layers, discovering new burns in unexpected places every time she was sure she was done with all that. "I don't want to go back to the apartment anyway." That dingy apartment she and Nicky rented now seemed so unbearably *temporary*. They couldn't see the river, and they seemed far away from everyone. It was the worst of both worlds. Stuck in the middle, endlessly coping.

Keeping her life on hold while her candy store was rebuilt choked Jeannie like smoke.

"I figure you've got five more minutes of old business, then Chad will be up. Really, Jeannie, you don't have to be here." Abby caught Jeannie's eyes in the dingy gold-framed mirror above the sink. "So don't go home. Go shopping, go eat a pound of fudge, go walk over and sit by the river if you want, but give yourself a break and leave."

Abby made it sound as if Jeannie could slip out unnoticed. "Every single person in that room will know if I skip out. And they'll know why—Chad's the fire marshal and George is the fire chief. It couldn't be more obvious."

"So what?"

"Well..." Jeannie fished for a better reason than her stubborn defiance of a paralyzing fear. "If I leave, how will I know whatever it is George wants to say about Nicky?" She shut off the water with a resolute twist of the faucet. There was nothing for this but to do what she always did: fix her eyes on gratitude and soldier on. And on, and on. She'd worked at being grateful; she'd sent baskets of goodies to George and Chad and the rest of the volunteers at the fire department. *Sent,* because she still couldn't bring herself to go into the fire station. The least she could do—the goal she'd set for herself tonight—was to sit through the presentation, stay upright, force a smile and be grateful Chad Owens was as handsome as he was thorough.

Don't look at her. Chad Owens kept telling himself to keep his gaze away from Jeannie Nelworth. He shouldn't single her out in any way, but his eyes repeatedly wandered over to her tight smile no matter what he resolved. It was a hopeless cause; everyone in the room seemed overly aware of the woman.

Jeannie loved yellow, loved kids and normally exuded as much happiness as twelve people, but she looked pale and drawn tonight, cornered by the collective awkwardness. George kept putting his arm around her, looking out for her as if she needed shielding from the world. That was George, everyone's unofficial protective grandfather. The town's most beloved fire victim at a fire safety presentation—honestly, he was amazed she showed up at all.

Chad thought Jeannie should have some space after the presentation, an escape from the small tight knot of false casualness that pushed around her after the talk, but George motioned Jeannie out of the group right away, calling her over to where they were standing.

"How are you?" George hugged her. George hugged everyone.

"George," Jeannie said with an applied smile. "I am fine." She pushed her brown bangs out of her eyes like a nervous teenager. "Stop worrying, why don't you?"

"You know very well I won't. I'm looking out for you, so help me stop worrying by saying yes to my idea."

Jeannie rolled her eyes, crossing her hands over her chest. "How about I hear your idea first?"

George crossed his hands over his own chest and leaned in. "I want to hire Nick."

There was a momentary flash of panic in her eyes. "Don't you think thirteen is a bit young to be a firefighter?"

George laughed. "Every boy wants to be a fireman. But not every boy can be a fire-dog walker." He said it with an absurd importance Chad didn't feel and Jeannie clearly didn't believe.

Chad hadn't been in favor of George's scheme to hire Nick to walk the portly firehouse hound. Plug certainly needed exercise, but Chad found the gesture lacking. George should know better than to put a cozy bandage on a kid's enormous trauma. Fire stole something from a soul that could never be restored. Chad knew it. Nick and Jeannie knew it now, too, and some cuddly chore wouldn't make that go away. Still, no one talked George out of anything once he got a plan in that meddling, generous mind of his. Chad supposed the scheme couldn't hurt, but he didn't think it stood any real chance of helping.

"You have *volunteer* firefighters but you want to *pay* my son to walk your dog?" Jeannie's eyes narrowed with a friendly suspicion at the idea. Her long, dark ponytail swung as she gave George a sideways glance. Chad was glad Jeannie recognized George was up to something.

She wasn't pretty in the stop-a-guy-dead-in-his-tracks kind of way. It was more her energy, her optimism, that pulled people toward her. Those brown eyes always took in the world like it was a fantastic package waiting to be opened. Nothing seemed to keep her down. Last year she'd had her Jeep painted in the same yellow polka-dotted pattern as her store, and while all the other merchants thought it stunning marketing, all Chad could think about was how mortified her son must be to ride in the thing. Still, everyone in town knew Jeannie Nelworth's Sweet Treats candy store. Half the businesses in the county used her gift baskets, and the woman's chocolate-covered caramels were nearly legendary.

"Plug would be good for Nick," George lobbied, smiling as if every volunteer fire department had a dog-walking budget. "Boys love dogs."

Jeannie let out a sigh. "Well, Nicky seems to need to take care of something since…" Her voice fell off, as if she'd run out of good ways to end a sentence like that. Chad knew the feeling. He knew exactly how a life split forever into "before the fire" and "after."

"The guidance counselor suggested a pet," Jeannie continued with a hollow laugh, "But all our landlord allows is a goldfish. Those are 'lame,' as Nicky so bluntly put it."

Dr. Billings cut into their little trio. "So, Jeannie, how's our Nicky doing?"

"Really great." Jeannie gave the dentist a big smile. "People have been so kind."

They're always so kind, Chad thought. People were so kind after Laurie's death he thought he'd drown in careful kindness. Friends and family surrounded him with casseroles and cards and "how are you's" that hoped to avoid his sad answers. That was why it had been so easy to move here. Only George knew what he'd been through, why his history with fire went beyond the professional and into the personal. He kept him off the fire engines and at a desk; Chad liked his pain to stay private. People never looked at him the same way again once they knew, so he made sure no one did.

As for Jeannie, she had no choice. She was on display for everyone's pity because the *whole town* had gathered to watch her home and business burn. He was sure she'd call it something warm and cozy like "community," but to him it was a naked, painful exposure.

"Still, he's been through so much for such a young man." Billings patted Jeannie's wrist.

"Oh, don't you worry about Nicky. He's coping so much better than anyone expected. You know boys. He just sees this as a chance to get cooler new stuff. Like Christmas before Christmas. People came out of the woodwork to help us, you know. Nicky and I had a week's worth of clothes before the sun even came up the next day. The new Sweet Treats will be right on Tyler Street in the middle of all that lucrative tourist traffic. And evidently, my son is about to become the firehouse's first official dog wrangler."

"Told you she'd say yes." George elbowed Chad victoriously. "Have Nicky come by Chad's office tomorrow but don't tell him what's up. The boy will enjoy it more if it's a surprise."

"It will be bigger and better. It has to be," Jeannie proclaimed to the dust the following morning as she stood inside what would be Sweet Treats. It made her happy just to be inside the historic building, the "old girl" as Jeannie had come to call her. The weathered beams boasted deep ridges like laugh lines. History's scent, that indescribable mixture of dust and mold and time, hung in the air to the point where Jeannie felt she could reach out and roll it between her fingers. It was a thick, rich smell, but not unpleasant by any means. This old girl had gone unappreciated for far too long; she had too grand a history to sit dormant on Tyler Street. "How many times have the floodgates saved you?" The green floodgates at the north end of town were a Gordon Falls landmark, protecting the town from the nearby Gordon River when its fury swelled. "You've been a dozen different things, and now you'll be my candy store." Twenty-seven Tyler Street had been an apothecary shop back at the turn of the century, and then a pharmacy in the 1920s and 1930s back when pharmacies had ice cream counters and weren't giant chain stores. "You've got character. We both do."

She laughed at herself, holding conversation with wood and plaster. Still, the building and she were old friends of a sort. How many times had she passed by this neglected spot in such a prime location just across from the firehouse, pondering what she could do with it if she ever got the chance? Every couple of months, she'd slow down as she drove past it with its forlorn for-sale sign. She would toy with the idea that someday, when the timing and the finances were right, it might be time to expand, to leave the cramped quarters over by the river and make a go of it on Gordon Falls's center stage. She'd have enough space in here to really utilize her online gift basket business—growing fast enough, thank the Lord, to keep her going over this tough time. She'd been bursting out of her riverfront home and shop already. Now, being stuck in this apartment and borrowing the church's industrial kitchen to cook, wasn't going to cut it much longer.

Jeannie took a deep breath, watching the way the light striped through the dusty air. Though some details were lacking, she could feel her future in here. The whole enterprise still seemed steeped in possibility— one of the things that kept her going these days. Nicky had jokingly called the project "Mom's other baby." How glad he was that his mother found somewhere else to put her attention. He wasn't far off the mark. It felt as though if she didn't move forward at full speed, she'd stop all together. For the thousandth time she thought of the little sign she'd seen in the hospital lobby the night Henry died. It said, "You never know how strong you can be until strong is the only choice you have."

Jeannie ran her hands over beams and dusty shelves, drawing motivation from the possibilities. She'd have twice the room for stock in this place. She could have internet kiosks for customers to order for relatives and friends back home. Maybe even a class or two in that big side room off the kitchen. "I need you, you need me. We're business partners. God set it up that way and nothing is going to stop us now."

"Except maybe me, the insurance company and a handful of building codes," came a deep voice from behind her. Jeannie spun around, nearly yelping in a most unprofessional manner, to find Chad Owens standing in what would be the front doorway.

Chapter Two

A set of blueprints she'd bumped began to cascade off the folding table, and Jeannie just managed to save them from a swirl of dust. "I didn't hear you come in." She started to say that just because the building didn't have a working door didn't mean a person shouldn't knock, but kept quiet. Chad would make Nicky happy later this afternoon, if George's plan worked, so she shouldn't complain. Besides, she figured it would be wise to stay on good terms with the fire marshal when rehabbing a eighty-seven-year-old building on a tight time schedule.

"Obviously." Chad wore a dark green turtleneck that wouldn't have looked half as severe on any other man. He never dressed starkly—mostly like a man who never put much thought into how he looked—but somehow everything about him managed to have sharp edges. Even his green eyes, which currently held an unsettling hint of amusement, flashed more murky than mossy under his short, dark hair. "Do you always talk to empty rooms?"

"Henry used to say I could think only with my mouth moving." She'd always thought it funny but now it just sounded foolish.

"Your late husband?"

It startled her that he had to ask; everyone in town knew Henry. Had Chad really not been in Gordon Falls long enough to have known him? "Yes. We lost him in a car accident when Nicky was six." It felt odd to realize someone she knew hadn't known Henry. As if it signaled just how long Henry had been gone.

His stance softened a bit at her answer, as if tripped up by the tragedy. Chad was as athletic as any of the firemen he worked with, but he moved like a man who would have preferred to take up less space in the world. If he ever got excited about anything, she'd never seen it.

Well, she wouldn't allow him to do his wet-blanket routine in this place this morning. She pointed to the amazing woodwork near the top of the walls. "Isn't this moulding incredible? It's artwork. Why would anyone think covering up such craftsmanship with one of those boring industrial drop ceilings was a good idea? Outlaw *that* in one of your building codes."

"Some people think new is better, no matter what." Chad looked up at the partial latticework of steel strips that had held up one of those horrid 1970s foam-tile ceilings and scratched his chin. His strong features could have been dashing if his personality would just lighten up, but he always seemed rather sad. He followed her gaze up to the wondrously curvy wood moulding. "Scraping the old paint off all those curlicues won't be an easy job."

Jeannie palmed the fat arc of a wooden support column, ignoring his pessimism. The store had six thick columns running down each side of the long narrow shop. They were stately things no one ever put in buildings anymore. When she was finished, each column would bear rounds of wrought-iron display baskets, brimming with salt water taffy and her famous chocolate-covered caramels; a forest of sweetness down either side of the aisle. "Oh, I won't scrape those," she said, pointing upward. "I love the texture of all those layers. All those years, all that history. They'll be stunning when I paint them up in bright colors."

Chad simply stared at the ceiling with his hands in his pockets. She wondered, by the tilt of his chin, if he was trying to see what she saw. Perhaps he was just categorizing her as a loony optimist, a thorn in his side as the fire marshal and building inspector who had to sign off on all her ambitious remodeling plans. He surveyed the entire ceiling before bringing his gaze down to her with narrowed eyes. "Are you going to paint all the exposed ductwork up in bright colors, too? The sprinkler pipes and such?"

Jeannie leaned against the beam, wincing as it groaned a bit. The late-September wind whistled through something behind her, announcing the gap-toothed age of the windows and doors. She spoke over the sound. "Of course. I'm going to paint *everything* bright colors."

He sighed, a sound considerably more weary than the building's aged whistle. "I was afraid of that."

"You don't see it? The energy, the kids on

summer vacation, the tourists buying goodies for their family back home? The noisy students after school and on Saturday mornings?" It was so clear to her, she couldn't imagine anyone not picturing the vivid image.

"I see outdated plumbing and old wires and no sprinkler system. I see a whole lot of work, frankly."

"You've no imagination." She sighed. "That's sad."

"I'm paid to see exactly what's there. That's safety."

The insurance adjuster was going to be here any minute, and Jeannie wasn't going to let Chad Owens rain on her parade. Not today. Jeannie set about unrolling the blueprints, weighting down its curling corners with the thermos of coffee and box of cookies she'd brought for the meeting. "You don't have to set foot in here once you've signed off on my permit," she called over her shoulder as she heard Chad's boots traveling the floor with calculated, assessing steps. "You don't ever have to cross over from your dark and gloomy side of the street if you don't want to."

Chad stopped and looked at her. "Dark and gloomy?"

"I wasn't talking about the decor." In fact, the fire station across the street was another local landmark, a majestic stone castle with bright red trim on the windows and a trio of enormous red doors. The Gordon Falls Volunteer Fire Department stood as a hub of activity and civic pride. Lots of people loved the firehouse, as she had before her association with the place became a little *too* personal. She used to be the kind of person who loved candles, too, but now she couldn't even strike a match. There was a reason she was bricking up the fireplace in here.

"I'm sorry," she conceded, shooting up a quick prayer to God for a bigger helping of grace this morning. "It's just that, while I'm all for safety, you know you can be a bit of a glass-half-empty kind of guy sometimes." *All the time,* she silently added.

"You think I'm the kind of person who'd pull over Santa's sleigh on Christmas Eve if I saw a taillight out."

"If I believed in Santa. And that sleighs had taillights."

He squared his stance at her. "It's my job to be careful. I take it very seriously, and you should be glad that I do. Here's the last of the forms you need to file for the occupancy permit. You can have Nick bring them over when he comes this afternoon to…start his job." He said that final part with an air of endurance.

Even though the answer was clear on his face, Jeannie asked, "What do you think of George's scheme?"

"I think George means well." He swallowed the rest of this thought, she could tell. "But…"

"But only time will tell if it's a good idea. If it helps."

Nicky just needed something to do, something to take care of—no one thought of this as some kind of home-remedy therapy. Of course it would help. "He'll love it. Plug needs it as much as Nicky. More, actually."

"He's a fat dog, I'll grant you that. As for the rest of it…" She didn't like the look in his eyes as he let the sentence hang in the air unfinished. He handed her the papers she needed for the adjuster and turned to go. *You'd better let me in on what You're doing here, Lord,* she prayed as Chad closed the door, *because I can't see how Nicky and Chad will ever get along.*

* * *

George looked up from the hose he was inspecting, making Chad realize he'd let the firehouse door slam harder than necessary. "So," George said with a smirk, "how are things at the Big Rock Candy Mountain?" As last night's dog-walking proposition had proven, George kept his hands in every aspect of Gordon Falls's community life. He kept his nose in the lives of each and every one of his volunteer firefighters, too. The younger firefighters loved George. His grandfatherly personality was half the reason Gordon Falls hosted a volunteer fire corps. People would do anything to help the guy.

"I think you're nuts with this dog thing."

"But you'll go along with it, right?"

Chad *would* do anything to help George— except climb a ladder again, although he'd been known to pitch in during extraordinary circumstances. George never questioned Chad's decision to "chain himself to a desk," even though he disagreed with the choice. They had too many mutual secrets not to defend each other. Chad was one of the few people who knew the now-widowed George even had a son. Clark had been a colleague of Chad's back during his early fire-fighting days, but the Bradens men hadn't spoken to each other in almost ten years. Stubborn as oxen, the pair of them. Despite the fact that Clark had somehow managed to refer Chad to this position here in Gordon Falls, Chad never could get either man to divulge the source of the wedge between them. He and George understood each other's private wounds, respected them and had developed a father-son relationship of their own.

"That place is going to be a riot of color. And loud." Chad set down the clipboard he'd taken over to Jeannie's, pausing to scratch Plug. "Jeannie Nelworth is optimistic to a fault."

"What a surprise," George grunted as he wrestled the massive section of hose onto its shelf. "Still, everything's in order?"

"Yes." Chad finished with Plug and stepped over the dog to help George work another section into stiff coils. George was well past the age other fire chiefs retired. He ought to be sitting at the diner arguing with Gordon Falls's other grandpas, fishing on the river and populating church spaghetti dinners, not coiling hoses. Still, stubborn old George refused to even consider the notion of stepping down.

"That's not a very convincing yes."

"She needs to be more cautious. That's an old building and she's gonna have mobs of kids in there every afternoon."

George pushed his ever-present baseball hat back on his head, showing his balding mop of now-more-white-than-red hair. "This is a woman who's just survived a fire, Chad. You of all people know what that does to a person. Go easy. I have no doubt she'll go the extra mile so all those cute little tykes can stay safe buying their bubblegum. She's just raw right now, and she needs to move forward to feel better. Take a little extra care walking her through the process, will you?"

Chad scowled. Extra care was George's department, not his. It was George who stuffed himself into the firehouse's Santa suit for every Christmas party, George who'd found Plug as a stray puppy and took him in despite serving no clear use short of good company. Which begged the question he'd been wanting to ask George since yesterday: "So why draft *me* into overseeing Nick as Plug's official dog walker?"

"Your sunny disposition, of course."

With a whistle Plug would ignore, George walked out of the equipment bay into the firehouse kitchen to pull open the refrigerator. "You can relate to the boy, I think. He needs watching. And you? You've been gloomier than usual. I know October's coming, but…"

"Don't." Chad hated it when George got it into his head to play armchair shrink.

The old chief sighed. "It's been eight years, Chad. That's too long to play hermit, don't you think?" George pulled out a brown glass bottle of root beer and snapped its cap against the bottle opener mounted nearby.

Chad moved in front of him. "So I need a thirteen-year-old? To supervise? This is a bit off the mark, even for you."

"You're just like Nick. You need something other than your losses to care about. And goldfish *are* lame."

"George…"

Ignoring his challenge, George took a healthy swig followed by a satisfied sigh, then gazed out the kitchen window onto Tyler Street. "He's a great kid, but he's been through too much. The way I see it, you know something about holding up that kind of weight. And since you won't go full-time back onto an engine, you've got too much free time."

George could be exasperating when he hatched a plan, but Chad knew better than to argue with him. He didn't care one bit for the orchestrating look in George's eye as they stood in silence for a moment, staring across Tyler Street to Jeannie's shop. A pair of work lights strung from the high ceilings of Jeannie's shop gleamed out through the front windows on either side of the boarded-up doorway like yellow eyes over a square wood nose. Her yellow polka-dotted Jeep was still out front, but the blue insurance van had driven off. Jeannie was probably still in there, cooing to the woodwork with visions of sugarplums dancing in her head.

"I don't want to do this, George."

"Well, I suppose I can't make you, either."

Oh, I suspect you can. "She bothers me. You should see the colors she's gonna paint that place. It'll be like working across the street from a life-size game of Candy Land."

"It will, won't it?" George chuckled. "It'll be nice to see that building full of life again, don't you think? My dad used to take me over to that store for root-beer floats when I was Nick's age. Best treat in the world. Not like all the sugar water they call soda pop now." George's beefy hand came down onto Chad's shoulder. "Don't be the guy to stop Jeannie Nelworth from reopening her candy store for the holidays. It'd be giving the Grinch a run for his money."

"She's got to be careful."

"She'll *be* careful, Chad. She's got more reason to be careful than all of us put together with what she's been through. I'm kind of proud of her, actually, getting back into the swing of things so quick and taking on such a big project like this. She's got spirit, that woman. Can't knock Jeannie Nelworth down for long."

That was it. The fact that Jeannie Nelworth was so unsinkably cheerful, that she bobbed right back up after every blow like some over-buoyant bath toy was *exactly* what bothered him about her.

Chapter Three

~~~

The restaurant down the street had blocked its secondary exit with a Dumpster again. Why didn't some of these businesses take his inspections more seriously? A knock on his door startled Chad out of his paperwork. He looked up from the report he'd been writing to see Nick Nelworth standing in his doorway. "Hey, Mr. Owens. Chief Bradens said you had something to ask me."

Jeannie's son had that legs-too-long amble of every teenager, but it was the way he always hung his head that caught Chad's attention. George was right; life had beaten Nick down a lot more than the boy would let on. The kid had lost his dad to a car crash in the first grade, and then his home had burned—all before he even hit everything high school would throw at him. How could Nick hope to have anything but a dark outlook on life, even with his mother's high-voltage optimism? From what Chad remembered, mothers and thirteen-year-old sons barely spoke the same language as it was.

He didn't really know Nick, hadn't known him at all before the fire, but felt an instant recognition now. Anyone could easily see the kid was quietly unhappy. And why not? Chad recalled hating every minute of middle school, and he'd had none of Nick's traumas to overcome. Annoyed as he was at George's scheming, Chad couldn't tamp down an urge to help the boy. "Hi there, Nicholas. How's it going across the street?"

Nick rolled his eyes—those same big eyes of his mother's. "Mom's all weird about it. She's talking really fast and forgetting where she put things."

The image of Jeannie Nelworth bouncing around her store hadn't left his mind since the meeting. "Your mom's excited about the place?"

"Yeah, something like that." Plug wandered in, nuzzling Nick's hand. "Whoa, Plug, that doesn't belong to you. Don't go getting Mr. Owens's forms all slobbery." Nick raised his hand out of Plug's reach—which didn't take much effort, because Plug never jumped up for anything—and put the handful of forms on Chad's desk. "Mom said to give you these…and these." He reached into his back pocket and reluctantly produced six very bright, very sparkly yellow pens. The promotional kind with "Sweet Treats" written on them in the pink swirly script that was Jeannie's logo. Nicholas looked about as eager to be handing those out as Chad would be to use them. "They have the new address on them and the website." He said in the monotone of a boy repeating an instructed script. Chad wondered if there was anything more repugnant to a thirteen-year-old boy than to be the distributor of sparkly pens.

Chad scooped the pens up, noting with horror that yellow glitter came off onto his fingers. "They're very…yellow." He raised an eyebrow at Nick, hoping to let the boy know he wasn't expecting an endorsement of anything so *cute*.

"Yep." Plug began inspecting Nick's hand and back pocket, evidently thinking glitter might prove tasty. "They are."

Chad slid out of his chair and came around to the front of his desk. He squatted down to scratch Plug between the ears. "Can you keep a secret?" Nick hunched down as well, and Plug rolled over on cue, to make sure they didn't miss scratching his big belly. "Don't tell your mom, but I'm not a fan of glitter. On anything."

The boy's eyes widened, then narrowed in a laugh. "Me, neither." Hadn't Jeannie given a thought to what a boy's life was like surrounded by all those perky pastels?

"Perfectly understandable. Not that I have to ask, but man-to-man, what's your position on yellow polka dots?"

The boy looked as if he were asked to reveal state secrets. "You mean Mom's car?" he nearly whispered. After a long pause where both of them looked at the offending vehicle, Nick said, "Someday I'm gonna have to learn to drive in that thing."

Chad could feel Nick's embarrassment even as he tried to hide it. He was a grown man who never cared what people think, and he'd surely hesitate to climb into Jeannie Nelworth's Jeep. He was surprised to discover his hand had landed on the boy's shoulder. "I feel your pain, kid." He said it in a teasing tone, but he actually meant it. He wanted Nick Nelworth to know one person understood his predicament and how hard the world was as a thirteen-year-old boy. "Maybe we can talk her down a couple of shades by the time you hit fifteen."

Nick laughed. "Man, I hope."

The more relaxed look on Nick's face refused to let Chad keep his distance. Kids were not his strong suit. He gave the safety talks every year at school and did the driver's ed pre-prom speech about drinking and driving, but that was more because he had the time to do these things. With all the other crew volunteers, he viewed this as payback for staying off the engines. Not only that, but life had handed him too many reasons to make fire prevention a personal cause.

But this? Even George had to know this one-on-one teen stuff was way out of Chad's job description. "Plug's getting too fat, even for him." He rubbed the hound's round belly, eliciting a lazy canine moan of satisfaction. "He needs more exercise, don't you think?"

"He's pretty big, that's for sure."

"Plug needs to walk off a few pounds, wouldn't you say? How many days a week are you free after school?"

"I've got math club Tuesdays and Thursdays, but nothing the other days."

"George and I are too busy to give Plug any regular exercise. Do you think you could help us out by walking him? Twice a week, maybe? For pay, of course…say, seven dollars a week?" Plug was George's dog, technically. George should be doing this. Chad should not be anywhere near this, and yet here he was and nearly glad of it, besides.

"I think. That is, if Mom says it's okay. She's gonna be up here every day working on the store, anyway."

Chad tried to ignore Nick's eyes, and what they did to the spot below his throat. He stood up before something stupid came out of his mouth. "George already asked your mom. You're hired. When can you start?"

"Now." Nicholas shot up beside him. "I could start right now."

"I had a feeling you'd say that. Which is why I happen to have Plug's leash right here on my desk." Chad nudged the hound with his foot. "With this kind of enthusiasm, we'll get you fit and trim in no time, Plug."

Nick attached the leash after giving Plug a friendly scratch under the chin. When he looked at Chad again, the boy's face was the complete opposite of the bored reluctance it had been when he first entered the office. George would never let him forget how right he'd been about the idea of hiring Nick Nelworth.

"Thanks. We're off!" With a wave, Nick trotted out of the office door with a slightly confused Plug lumbering behind him. From the window he could see Nick stood up straighter, walked without most of that lanky teen shuffle and generally looked delighted. Plug even went so far as to wag his tail—something Chad hadn't seen in months.

He thought they'd take off up the street, but evidently their first stop was across the street to Sweet Treats. If Chad's guess was right, Sweet Treats would start carrying dog biscuits when it opened, and Plug would be a regular customer.

The next day, Jeannie sat in the front window of Sweet Treats. She wasn't calling it "the building that would become Sweet Treats" anymore, for the space had already become the store in her mind. She was assessing how a stack of yellow paint chip choices looked in the afternoon sun. Buttercup definitely outshone Sun-kissed, but

Lemon had a vitality to it she couldn't resist. She'd nearly settled on "Lemon"—it was a candy flavor, after all—when a lumbering movement out of the corner of her eye drew her attention. Plug was sauntering across Tyler Street by himself.

It only took a second or two to figure out Plug's motives; his red leash—the dog's only nod to the classic firehouse Dalmatian—was clamped firmly in his slobbery jaws and he was heading straight for Sweet Treats. A determined, albeit slow-motion quest for Nicky. Jeannie couldn't help but laugh at the sight. Sure, Nicky had told her he and Plug really enjoyed their walk yesterday, but Plug obviously hadn't checked the clock to know Nicky wasn't due out of school for another hour.

Her laughter turned to a gasp when a car whizzed by too close behind Plug. He swiveled his head after the speeding car, but didn't seem to register the possible danger of being out in traffic. Had the hound ever been in the street other than watching the engines come and go from the firehouse? She could count on one hand the number of times she'd even seen him moving. Mostly Plug sat still, as he was doing now. Only now he just stood in the middle of the street, staring into her doorway as if willing Nicky to appear there.

When a second car went by, barely slowing down as it slipped between her shop and Plug, Jeannie sucked in a breath and moved. Opening her door, she called, "Go on home, Plug," and pointed back to the firehouse. The trio of big red engine bay doors were shut. How had he gotten out? "Get back out of the street before you get hit."

Plug cocked his head to one side in an all-too-human gesture of bafflement. "Plug, go home!" Jeannie found herself enunciating as if to a small child or someone who didn't understand English. This was why she'd never owned a dog—you could never reason with a pet. Unreasonable sons were just about all she could handle right now. "Home, boy!"

While he didn't sit down, he didn't turn to go home, either. Plug just stood there, as if waiting for her to catch on that he had no plans to cut his excursion short, escorted or not.

Jeannie looked up and down the street, hoping to catch one of the volunteer firemen out looking for him. Gordon Falls boasted a full complement of volunteer firefighters, but

George and Chad were often the only two in the building. Those on call only came rushing when those horrid sirens went off because that's how a volunteer fire department worked.

Still, shouldn't *someone* have noticed Plug leaving? Seeing another car heading down the street, Jeannie realized she was the only one to come to the poor hound's rescue. Even though she wasn't quite sure what to do, Jeannie settled on squatting down and tapping her knee the way she'd seen Nicky call him. "Well, fine then. You come here. Come, Plug. Come on, boy. Come on over here and get your fool self out of the street." Plug took two steps toward her. "Come on, boy!" She'd let the dog stay here for the hour until Nicky could deliver him back over if the firefighters didn't come looking for him first. She surely had no plans to walk out there and haul him back to the firehouse herself.

No, sir, she would not haul Plug back herself. She couldn't stomach the thought of walking to the firehouse for any reason, much less a dog. Today was not the day to tackle her fear.

Other people found the red doors charming; iconic, even. Every time Jeannie looked at those huge red doors, they just seemed like hungry red mouths opening wide to eat her alive. Nope, she wouldn't face those today.

"That's right, come on over here and you can wait for Nicky." At Nicky's name, Plug picked up the pace to something that could almost be called a trot, finishing his trek across Tyler Street. He looked up at her with that comical face of his, those too-big eyes and those floppy ears, and announced his arrival by dropping the leash on the sidewalk in front of her. Then, after a pathetic growly sound which she suspected loosely translated to "Phew!" he placed his big nose on her knee and depositing a dark spot of drool on her pant leg. "You silly old thing," she said, unable to stay annoyed once she started petting his massive, velvety ears. "Don't you know enough to stay out of traffic?"

She didn't like the look Plug gave her in response. His droopy eyes seemed to say "Silly yourself if you can't walk across the street to take me home."

"Oh, no you don't," she countered. "You're not tricking me into..." Into what? Doing the thing she'd managed to avoid for weeks now? She could sit through a presentation on fire safety but couldn't set foot in a firehouse? Who really was the silly old thing here?

No, Lord, I'm not ready. Jeannie knew she was being ridiculous, even irrational, but the thought of going near the firehouse stirred up panic in her throat. She didn't want to be this way. She'd tried being logical, thinking of "fire safety" as a worthy community goal, but that only made things worse.

Fire was the enemy. There had been a fire during her husband Henry's death in a car accident, as well. Looking at the aftermath of her house fire became just like being at the crash site the morning after Henry died.

I've been strong lots of other places. I even bought this place looking right at the fire station—wasn't that strong? After all, weren't these men the reason she had the ability to start over?

"You know it's no accident you chose this building," Abby had declared the day Jeannie signed the mortgage papers. "Some part of you needs the firehouse nearby."

"So why am I scared to have it so close? It makes no sense."

"You didn't make much sense before the fire," Abby had replied, hugging her. "I'm expecting less now."

For five whole minutes she tried to ignore Plug's stare, to let him wait until Nicky got home. *I don't have to go in there, not yet. Not for a dog, of all things.*

She parked herself back on the window-sill and attempted a return to the paint chips. Nothing worked; her concentration had fled the building. She was going to have to go in there *sometime*. If not today, it'd have to be some day. Wouldn't it be better to get it over with when Nicky wasn't watching? That way, she'd have an hour or so to pull her-self together if things were…harder than she planned. Then when Nicky showed up she could tell him how much Plug had missed him and how brave she'd been to take him back over. This was the perfect opportunity.

If she could just make herself take it.

She reached for the phone to call Abby for moral support, but put it back down. *You can do this. You are stronger than this.* Jeannie grabbed the leash, telling the pulse hammering in her throat to stop pounding so hard. This was a silly fear, the kind of thing she'd chide Nicky for having. No one should ever be afraid of a firehouse. Or fire engines. They meant help was on the way, didn't they?

"Fears don't make sense," the school counselor had told Nicky. "That's why you must simply face them. You can't argue them down because they won't listen to reason."

"All right, then, Plug my boy, it's time to get over this." Strong words, but her voice wobbled as she stood up and fastened the leash to his collar with shaking hands.

"Just walk you back on over there as if it's the easiest thing in the world. Right. Piece of cake."

Before she could gather another bolstering breath, Plug loped off the curb and began walking. As if this had been his plan all along.

"Yep, we're just walking across the street, taking you back home." Talking to Plug somehow kept her breathing. "Home to the nice, clean, safe firehouse with all the big… huge…loud…red engines."

Sounds from the fire—her fire—returned unbidden and unwelcome. Her head filled with the rumble of the engines. The noise had been so loud she felt it in her chest that horrible afternoon. The lifelike twitching and hissing of the hoses as the men fought to direct those gallons of water into the smoke pouring out of *her* home. The sour, sharp smell of her possessions burning, the cascading cracks of timber as her life collapsed in on itself. The running and shouting and the crunch of thick-gloved hands that kept moving her out of the way. The coaxing voices forcing her back when she wanted to plunge into the smoke after all the precious, precious things disappearing in front of her eyes. Worst of all was the crushing feeling of Henry's memory burning with the house they had shared. She'd lost so many precious things, but the cruelest result of all was how she could fit all the surviving mementoes of Henry into a single shoebox. Without souvenirs and photographs, how would Nicky ever remember his father clearly? Videos capturing his voice and gestures were gone. His teaching notes from his physics professorship at the local state university were now ash in the wind. How could a young boy remember the best part of a man, his strong soul or the way he loved life? She could barely picture Henry's handwriting now, and it tore her to pieces.

Jeannie shook her head, willing the storm of pain away. She was safe, alive, walking in the September sunshine. *Stay beside me, Lord. I'm safe now, You've seen to that. Help me. Help me face this last fear so Nicky and I can go on.* The prayers were coming in spurts with every step across the street. Plug tugged her forward, and Jeannie forced herself to feel the sunlight on her face, imagined God leading Plug leading her. *Stay close. Help me. Nearly there. Stay close.*

She fixed her gaze on Chad's office door, where it felt safer to head rather than the big red doors. The office door pulled open, framing Chad's surprised face in the doorway. She had to remind herself the surprise was for Plug's "breakout." He couldn't possibly imagine how hard it was for her to simply walk his dog across the street. No one but Abby knew of that fear. If she could manage the last few feet, maybe no one else ever would.

Chapter Four

Chad couldn't help but stare at Jeannie as she walked across the street. Her back was ruler-straight, her jaw tense even as she talked—to whom? Plug? The woman was quite obviously frightened to death of something. Was she terrified of dogs? She had the look of a soul walking into doom itself, forcing her feet into stiff, hesitant steps and clutching Plug's leash as if it were a lifeline. Her eyes locked on her destination—his door at first, and then on him once he opened it.

Those eyes made part of him want to rush out to meet her, but the sheer terror in them froze the other half of him to the spot. He had to do something, so Chad held out a cautious, encouraging hand as he called Plug. It seemed best to let Plug pull her across rather than going out to meet her.

"Almost there." She was close enough to be heard now as she squeaked the words. "Here we go, back to the firehouse where you belong." Chad couldn't rightly say if she was coaxing the dog or herself. He called to Plug again, hoping to hurry the dog, but Plug merely ambled along as if nothing were out of the ordinary. As if the hound were granting Jeannie the pleasure of a leisurely walk.

Searching for some way to help, Chad suddenly remembered he'd tucked a dog biscuit in his pocket five minutes ago when he'd discovered Plug was gone. Food was the only thing sure to quicken Plug's steps. He squatted down to Plug's eye level, pulled out the biscuit and waved it enticingly. "Come on, old boy, pick up the pace. I've got a biscuit just waiting." Plug sniffed the air, gave a hearty "woof" and perked up his ears.

Chad was thinking it worked, until a metal scream split the air.

Plug had realized it an instant before Chad did, he always did. As if he remembered what Chad had momentarily forgotten: the school fire drill. And not just any drill, but a full test of the volunteer company's response time so that the firehouse roared to life behind him and Plug surged out of Jeannie's grasp. She made this awful sound, a gasping sort of yelp, as the bay doors lifted and the siren continued to signal the test run.

Chad was supposed to be observing the company's departure while George stood at the school observing their arrival. Despite the fact that it had been planned for weeks, this was the absolute worst scenario for someone like Jeannie. Plug galloped past him, nearly knocking him down while Jeannie stood rigid with fear right in the path of the engines.

She couldn't stay where she was; the engines would be pulling out any second. Chad bolted out into the street, ignoring the sound she made as he grabbed her shoulders. She actually resisted him, stunned as she was with fear, but he pulled her off balance and threw an arm around her torso, dragging her away from the thunder as the firefighters started the engines. She was so small in his arms, and she was shaking fiercely—her chest heaving. More volunteer firefighters would be swarming over the station within seconds, and he would have picked her up and carried her out of the way if she fought him further.

As it was, Jeannie stumbled a bit but clutched at him as he dragged her out of the street. Forgetting his supervisory duties, Chad pulled her away from the bay doors and into his office, kicking the door shut behind him in a futile effort to muffle the sound. That sound. Even when he knew it was coming, the shriek of the siren could still send ice through his veins. "It's a drill," he shouted above the roar. "There's no fire.

"Just a drill, Jeannie," he repeated loud enough for her to hear. "You know the school has them every September. Everyone is safe." At the mention of the word *school,* Jeannie whipped her face around toward him. He didn't think it was possible for her eyes to go wider. Around him he heard the sound of volunteers climbing into gear and radio chatter. He was shirking his duties, but she mattered more right now. The siren's pitch finally descended as he guided her to his office chair, and as she collapsed into it. Once the siren fell silent, he heard her pulling in gulps of air like she'd just been dragged from the river. He'd never seen her undone like this; it made him crazy with worry that she'd faint. Getting down on his haunches in front of her, he kept his voice low and steady. "Jeannie, are you all right?"

She just shook her head, looking down.

"It's the middle school fire drill. We're using it this year to evaluate the company's response time. That's why everyone's running out." Suddenly, Chad put the pieces together. She was afraid of the station. Since buying the building, she'd never once crossed the street. And Jeannie Nelworth visited everybody. Despite Nick's many visits and even the baskets he knew she sent over, Jeannie herself had never set foot in the firehouse. Until today. How cruel was that? "I'm sorry you had to be here for this, Jeannie. I..."

"Why didn't I know?" She cut in, looking up with anger. "Someone should have told us. Nicky isn't ready for fire trucks to come screaming into the school parking lot. He needs to be ready."

"If everyone knows it's coming, it's not much of a test."

The fear in her eyes turned to fire. "So it's *okay* to scare my son out of his wits on account of *procedure?* Did you have to plan that test for *that* school this year? Oh,

Nicky." She clutched a hand to her chest. Her fingers were actually shaking.

Chad heard the metallic rumble of the huge equipment doors shutting. In the distance, the engine sirens died down and Chad could envision firefighters climbing out of their trucks calmly while teachers and students stood in lines on the school field. And he could just as easily imagine Nick standing, breathing hard and wide-eyed like Jeannie had just been, fighting to look calm while his insides were going off like firecrackers. George had suggested moving the company drill to the high school, but Chad had declined. He, who of all people knew what this might do to Nicky, had tried not to single the boy out in any way but had chosen wrong. "I'm sorry." The words seemed weak and too late, the quieting firehouse a condemnation of all the commotion and noise he'd sent Nick's way.

Jeannie rose, then squinted her eyes tight and let out a breath. "Ugh. No, wait. I'm sorry, this isn't your fault."

He was impressed that she was trying to smooth this over, and it only served to make him feel worse. "No, this *is* my fault. George wanted to move the drill to another school, or even pull this test off the school drill, but I thought it would be worse to do anything special to single Nick out." It sounded like the worst decision ever when he said it out loud. "And I was wrong."

It was a funny thing; he could see her apply that parental control thing mothers had, could actually see her pull herself together for Nick's sake. Normally he didn't see those things in people, but her emotions were obvious to him somehow. "I should go over there right now."

Chad put a hand out, knowing instantly what she was up to and certain it would only make things worse. "You know, I'm not so sure that'd be a good idea."

Jeannie huffed and stepped around his hand. "Of course it is. He's probably panicked out of his mind right now."

Chad had never been a parent, but he had been a thirteen-year-old boy. Despite not having enough sense to move the drill, Chad *did* have enough sense to remember that someone's mom coming to the rescue would be instant humiliation in middle school. He owed Nick the only thing he could still do—delay the boy's mother until she calmed down enough not to make a scene. Maybe even keep her from showing up at all. He grabbed the doorknob before she could reach it. "Even if he is upset—and yes, it's my fault if he is—you rushing in to scoop him up is only going to make things worse in front of his friends."

Any fear in her face was now replaced by a fierce, protective glare. "That's out of line. You're not his mother."

"No, I am not his mother. I botched this, but let's leave it at that. If you go over there and make any kind of scene, you'll just make my bad call a worse situation."

"I wouldn't make a scene."

He looked at her. She was a loving mother. She'd most definitely make a *big* scene. It was what loving mothers did. It was part of what made being thirteen so wonderful and awful at the same time—that much he remembered vividly. "You wouldn't? Really?" He pointed down at her clenched fists.

"Okay." She unclenched her hands, a tiny bit of the tension easing off her shoulders as well. "I might make a bit of a scene. I mean, look at me, I'm a mess already."

He couldn't help but smile just a bit. "Yes, but you know it's a drill now and you're *less* of a mess. I expect the same is true of Nick.

We threw him a curve, but he seems like a strong kid. Maybe we need to let him figure out a way to get over it on his own." He gestured toward the chair, and she sat down again. "If you like," he went on, grasping for any idea that might help, "I can call the guidance counselor in ten minutes. You know, see if everything went okay. I can casually mention Nick and see what she says. You and I can get a cup of coffee in the meantime and think of ways to punish Plug for his thoughtless escape." When she hesitated, he was surprised to hear himself add, "And maybe think of some way to reward you for making it across the street under dire circumstances." His tone of voice seemed to be coming from some other man. Some warm, friendly guy he didn't recognize. He disliked her stalwart optimism, but she fought so hard for it that he couldn't bring himself to fault her. "Coffee and ten minutes. Then you can boast to Nick about having made it across the street and into the firehouse for a whole ten minutes. Sirens included."

Her hand flew to her chest again, flattening up against the big, cream-colored fisherman's knit sweaters she wore. The thick weave made her seem even smaller, made the flush in her cheeks stand out all the more. "I don't think my pulse has come back down to normal yet."

Chad felt a grin take over his face before he could stop it. "In that case, maybe you shouldn't drink George's coffee."

Chapter Five

Chad made sure he was in the firehouse when Nick came over to walk Plug the next day. He also made sure Plug stayed in his office so he'd have a chance to see how the boy fared. No amount of remorse would shake responsibility for what he saw in Nick's blue eyes: the inner storm beneath his pose of teenage apathy. Yesterday obviously hadn't been the best of days for Nick. He was very glad to be here, but trying hard not to show it.

"So the fire drill was no big deal?" Chad made a careful effort to sound casual as he handed Plug's leash to Nick. He double-checked the file he was "reading," making sure he wasn't holding it upside down. He suspected Nick would linger in his office, and the boy had. Nick spent a few minutes playing with Plug, tussling with the hound in fidgety unease. Chad caught as many surreptitious glimpses as he could over the top of his file.

"It was a…bit…weird," Nick finally offered after a pause that was so long Chad had forgotten he'd asked a question. The boy busied himself with the leash. His hands stilled just a bit before he added, "Loud."

Chad pretended to need another folder from his filing cabinet, which meant he had to walk close to Nick. "That siren sure is loud, especially in here. If you're in my office when the siren goes off, it'll rattle your teeth." He snatched a glance at Nick and then shifted his gaze out the windows to Tyler Street. "Hey, I wonder if it rattles the windows in your mom's shop? Do you know?"

Nick forced out a bit of a laugh. "She jumps every morning at ten when you guys test the sirens. I don't know about the windows, but it rattles Mom, which is dumb because you do it every day. She knows it's coming."

So the boy sensed his mom's fear of the fire station. That made him doubly unlikely to tell his mother anything about yesterday, and Chad knew from the principal that yesterday hadn't gone well. Any other fire drill, and it would have been purely an internal school matter—no sirens, no fire trucks. Any other kid, and Chad might have waved it off as just a case of being in the wrong place at the wrong time. Chad wasn't one to poke his head into these kinds of things, but there was just something compelling about Nick Nelworth. For whatever reason, Chad wanted to help Nick if he could. Provided things didn't get messy or complicated.

Chad pretended to hold a receipt up to the light coming through the window. "She tell you Plug dragged her over here yesterday? In the middle of your fire drill?" He kept his voice as casual as if he were asking the weather.

He watched Nick's reflection through the window glass. He was surprised, which meant Jeannie hadn't told him of her escapade here. He wondered what that meant as he watched Nick think it over, too.

"You came looking for me, did'ya, boy?" Nick ruffled Plug's floppy ears, but made no comment about his mother. "I was in school and besides, I can't come by every day. At least not yet, anyway."

Chad turned around to face Nick. Plug was a big dog, and Nick was small for an eighth-grader, but he seemed especially small as he sat there on the floor of the office. Chad parked himself on the window ledge for a moment, letting himself enjoy their playful interaction. Plug's constant slobber didn't phase a thirteen-year-old in the slightest, and the dog came to life around Nick in a way Chad hadn't seen before. George was wise to put them together. "The whole thing was pretty funny, actually. Plug snuck out, near as I can tell. He carried his leash over to the shop and everything."

Nick pushed his forehead up against Plug's droopy eyebrows. "Did you do that, Plug? Did'ya?" Plug responded with a generous wet lick up Nick's cheek that sent the boy into giggles.

Chad ventured further. "You ought to be proud of your mom. It scared her to death to come over here with the sirens wailing but she made sure Plug got back home safe." That wasn't exactly how it happened, but close enough.

"She even freaks out whenever the sirens go off at home...at our *apartment*." Nick corrected himself with obvious distaste. "And we're four whole blocks away up the hill. She won't come over here. Well, she wouldn't come over here before." He caught Chad's eye. "Betcha she'll still say she sends me 'cause she's too busy, but it probably still creeps her out."

Chad had to tread very carefully here. He slid his weight off the windowsill and hunched down to Nick's level under the guise of finding a twig on the floor. "Probably still does. Sirens and fire engines do that to lots of people." He waited to see if that elicited some kind of response from the boy. When it didn't, he added, "I had a big fire happen to me...and a friend of mine...years ago and I still jump a bit when that thing goes off."

Chad never admitted that to anyone but George, and it felt risky to say it aloud even in his office. Still, it seemed like the best way to give Nick permission to admit that the sirens made *him* nervous, too. The boy said nothing, fiddling with the ID tags on Plug's collar as if he hadn't heard Chad's remark.

Chad let it sit for a moment, twirling the twig he'd picked up from the floor. Nick's guidance counselor, Mrs. Corning, had happened to be in the field near Nick during the fire drill—one of those things Laurie would have called a "God-incidence." While Mrs. Corning's initial report was good enough to keep Jeannie from barreling over to the school, a later call from her gave Chad reason to worry. Nick had held it together, but just barely. He'd been visibly shaken during the drill, argumentative in his next class and then quiet and sullen the rest of the afternoon in school.

"Plug howls at sirens," Chad tried again, just to see if the boy was listening. "Can you believe that?"

Now that they'd reached a safer topic, Nick looked straight at him. His eyes were as striking as his mother's, even though they were blue to Jeannie's brown. "He does? He howls?"

"Like a wolf. I suppose he thinks he's helping, but it's really pretty awful sounding. Stick around long enough, and you'll get a front-row seat to that show, although you may be sorry you did."

Chad hoped he'd opened up another window in the conversation, but got no response. There was little reason to be surprised. Hadn't he done the same thing himself? Whenever the topic of Laurie and the fire—or loved ones lost in fires, or loved ones lost at all—came up in conversation, Chad always shut down. It was just easier not to go there at all than to try and keep up some kind of "all better now" facade.

"Your mom still planning on opening up for the holidays?" That wasn't a safe topic of conversation, either. He'd lectured Jeannie about the size of the restoration she'd bitten off. The building she chose had been vacant for almost a dozen years. Most of the firefighters encouraged her, convinced Jeannie's shop would be an easy source of goodies once she opened, but Chad had reservations.

"Yep," Nick replied. "She says we'll have our own Christmas tree in our own place above the shop. I can't wait."

Chad stifled a sigh. Half the interior walls needed to be rebuilt, and if she did as much internet business as she said, she'd need a lot of rewiring. Given all that, Chad would put the mark closer to six months. He was trying to figure out what on earth to say when Nick quickly fixed the leash to Plug and stood up.

"Okay, we're gonna go out now."

So much for that opportunity. Nick wasn't going to offer up squat about what happened yesterday at school or how he felt about it.

Should Chad be glad it was over, or annoyed that he'd lost the chance to get the boy to open up? Since when did he care about getting young boys to open up, anyway?

Watching them stop at the corner, seeing Nick reach down and give the dog yet another pat, it was clear they would be good for each other, needed each other on some level. Somebody—canine or human, needed to pull the hurt out of that boy. Not that it was Chad's place to do it—the school had counselors for that. Still, something in the shadows of Nick's eyes grabbed a hold of Chad and wouldn't let go, as if the boy needed to escape and Chad held the only rope. He was still standing out the window, wondering how he could have been better at helping, when George came up behind him.

"Heard it didn't go so well yesterday," George said, staring at Nick and Plug.

Chad ran his hands down his face. "You were right. We never should have put Nick Nelworth through the full company showing up at his school. I messed up, George, and that poor kid paid the price." He stared after the unlikely pair as they headed down the sidewalk. A stumpy-legged hound loping happily after a gangly legged boy. Opposites, or maybe just complements. He suspected Nick took after his father in appearance, being light and tawny compared to his mother's dark and dramatic features. He'd never known Henry Nelworth, but people spoke of the fatal car accident with great sadness. Nick's late father had obviously been a good man, a great loss in that boy's life.

George peered down the street at the pair. "You were sticking to the rules. That's what you're paid to do, so don't beat yourself up. And you know, maybe it really was better not to make special arrangements. Nick had to get over that sometime, maybe sooner and all at once was better than later. He looks okay to me. He came back to the firehouse today without any trouble at all."

Chad knew the clinical signs of pediatric post-traumatic stress; they'd had classes on crisis care at the academy. He knew the signs of shock, the basics of first-responder interaction, the academic essentials of how fires affected children. This wasn't a clinical concern. It was more personal, an unwelcome, niggling feeling. Maybe it was just man-to-boy commiseration. He remembered the gawky confusion of middle school and hated to see any kid have something tragic like a house fire added on to that misery. Kids could be cruel at that age. "He's not all okay, George. I can see it."

"Well, if anyone could see it, it'd be you." He shot Chad a sideways glance. "You don't think I had you supervise our dog walker because of your sparkling personality, do you?" George had been wise enough to see he needed something, someone to care for and interact with. George was such a great judge of character, it still baffled him how the chief's own family could be so estranged from each other. Who knew how people messed up their relationships so easily? Maybe George had seen something in Chad that tugged at him the way that boy tugged at Chad.

George sighed. "Then there's Jeannie. Artie told me he was worried he'd have run her over if you hadn't pulled her out of the street."

The memory of Jeannie yesterday hadn't left him. He still couldn't shake the sight of her big eyes and her brittle, frozen stance as she clutched Plug's leash. The way she looked up at him from his office chair, fierce love for her son blazing in her features. "She was pretty upset, but I think she's okay."

George looked across the street and scratched his chin with the hand that wasn't holding a bottle of root beer. "Is she?" He hated it when George got all cryptic. Why was it that the old man could convey twelve sentences in two words?

He could see Jeannie bent over some papers on the table in her shop. "She looks okay to me."

George produced a disbelieving snort.

Chad turned to him. "What?"

"Oh, I'm sure it's nothing." George's fake sigh told otherwise.

"George, what?"

Taking a long slow sip, George turned back to eye Chad. "It's just that Ed from the hardware store called a bit ago."

"And said what?" What on earth did Ed have to do with any of this?

"Seems Jeannie Nelworth came in yesterday afternoon and bought eight smoke detectors."

"She doesn't need that many. Even with two stories, she needs four, maybe five. And they will be hardwired in that place once the interior walls go up anyway. She has no use for the hang-up kind you get at Ed's."

"Yep." With a long look at Chad that said entirely too much, George took another sip and left the room.

Chapter Six

"Push the red button and hold for ten seconds to test." Jeannie read the directions aloud the next morning as she snapped the sides of the smoke detector together shut after inserting the battery. "Sounds easy enough." With a deep breath, she counted to three and pushed the red button. In seconds a shriek blasted throughout the building. "Oww!" She fumbled to pull the battery back out. "That's bad enough to make your eyes water. If there ever was a fire here, they wouldn't just hear you at the firehouse, they'd hear you clear to Ohio," she addressed the disassembled device. "You go by the room that'll be Nicky's, because that boy sleeps like a rock."

She put the battery back in and pressed the

reset button. "One down." Jeannie let out the breath she held and started unpacking the other seven devices and their respective nine-volt batteries. They needed to be changed every six months according to the detector manual, but she was planning on changing them every three months, just to be safe.

A knock at the window revealed Chad Owens, holding an aerosol can and pretending to plug his ears. It was the closest thing to humor she'd ever seen from him. Despite his rare near-smile, it felt odd to see him again so soon after her…episode…at the firehouse. He'd seen something too private in her panic. The imbalance that she knew next to nothing about him only made it worse. Stumped for what else to do she pulled the "door" open and asked sheepishly, "So you can hear it over there?"

He didn't answer. Well, of course he heard it over there. He certainly wasn't here to buy candy or see Nicky.

"Look, I…" Not only couldn't she begin to explain *why* she'd bought all these, she didn't in the least want to defend the purchase. Not to him, anyway.

Chad, however, didn't seem to be here to lecture. As a matter of fact, the look on his face was almost warm. Understanding? From Chad Owens? She didn't know what to do with that, especially on top of how nice he'd been to her this week. The whole thing made her wildly uncomfortable and not a little embarrassed.

He managed a wobbly smile and pointed to the can labeled Canned Smoke. "In case you were wondering, just pressing the button isn't an effective test. Even a match won't do it. You need actual smoke."

"Well, that's a relief because I hate matches." Jeannie hadn't planned on admitting to the fire marshal that the sight of even a lit match made her nervous. Then again, she'd already gone way past nervous in front of him, hadn't she?

It was as if the green of his eyes cast a whole new color she'd never noticed before. "You know you don't need so many of these. You must know that." His voice was soft and careful, almost pained.

"I know that. Well, part of me does."

"That part doesn't always win, does it?" It was as if he somehow knew the wild impulse that had driven her to the hardware store, and didn't think it so crazy. "Technically, you don't even need one. The building will have a hardwired system and sprinklers." He held her gaze, and the room seemed to shrink close around them. "You saw the plans, you know that, too."

Yes, the logical side of her knew better, but fear wasn't about logic, and her panic in front of the firehouse had blindsided her with a force she hadn't felt since the fire. "I had to do something. Even if it was silly."

"The hardwired ones won't be installed for two weeks yet. You won't have your occupancy permit for some time. Wouldn't it be easier to just stay out of the building until the fire detection system is in?"

"I can't. I need to be in here now." Jeannie pointed toward the detectors, unable to break the lock of Chad's gaze. "This was the only thing that came to mind." It wasn't a perfect solution, but it was immediate, and she needed immediate. Immediately.

"You can't live in here without the occupancy permit. You can't really work here, either."

"I know that, too. I just need to be in here as much as I can."

An amused understanding played across his features. He gave her the first true smile she'd seen from him. A kind, you-know-better smile, the sort she'd give Nicky if she caught him doing his homework with the television on. After a long moment, he put the can down on the table. She must have done a poor job of hiding her relief, for he shook his head gently and began taking the next detector out of its packaging. "I put four in my mother's house one year."

How could he make fun of her like that? "I suppose you'll tell me it was after a devastating fire," she blurted out, agitated from feeling so exposed. "The one that drove you into a career in fire prevention or something like that?"

Where had that come from? Why had she burst out with something so flippant? Chad's body changed instantly, every ounce of warmth disappearing in a flash. He stilled for a bristling second, and she thought he'd surely pick up the can and leave. Instead, after a sigh, Chad continued opening another package with angry precision.

"I'm sorry," she groaned, filled with sharp regret at her outburst. She hadn't realized how the week's tension had worn her thin. Nicky was such a bundle of lay-off-me attitude when he came to meet her here yesterday that she'd nearly thrust him across the street to Plug rather than go home and be trapped in that tiny apartment with him. Still, nothing excused her behavior just now. "That was way out of line, Chad. Really. Forgive me."

Without looking up at her, he snapped a battery into its place in the device. "Actually, you hit it pretty close. You're not the first person to clean out the smoke detector aisle after a fire." He flicked his eyes up, and the pained understanding Jeannie saw there planted a lump in her throat. "Just the most... enthusiastic."

She sank down onto one of the store's big windowsills—the ones that would eventually overflow with sunny yellow cushions. "What happened?"

He continued working a second detector out of its packaging, and was on the third when he finally said, "It was a long time ago. Where I used to live, in Indiana."

She started to ask another question, but something told her to just stay silent. The size and quiet of the room seemed to soothe him as much as it soothed her. His hesitation told her this wasn't a story he told often, if ever.

"She loved leaves," he began, his eyes falling closed for a moment as if blocking out the pain. "She was a botanist for the parks department, and she was forever bringing dried leaves and foliage into her house."

"Who?" Jeannie asked as quietly as she could, even though it was written all over his face.

His hands stilled and Jeannie could watch him dredge the answer up out of somewhere deep in his chest. His throat worked, his shoulders tensed even as his hands rested on the box. "My fiancée."

The weight of those two words sucked the air right out of the room. He remained motionless for the longest of moments, and Jeannie wasn't sure if the two words had actually echoed through the empty building, or it had just felt as if they did. *My husband,* Jeannie said to herself, thinking of Henry. *The other half of me, the person at the center of my world.* Jeannie knew the massive quality of that loss. The sorrow behind those two words made it easy to see why Chad was such a quiet man. She stared at him, aching, but he did not look up. He swallowed hard, and she saw his fingers flex briefly into fists before he reached across the table for a battery and snapped it into place.

"I'm so sorry." The reply felt weak and useless. "I'm…" There was no point in trying to find adequate words. She, of all people, knew there weren't any.

Chad looked up at her, and it was as if the dusty air swirled around their combined grief. She'd known him for two years, but could never see him the same way again, knowing what she knew now. What she'd mistaken for distance was really that "constant sorrow," the songs spoke of, the sharp press of grief she knew all too well. His pain was plain as day to her now. How had she not seen it before?

All her annoyance with him at this meeting or that, cautioning a committee about potential danger, and his reputation as "a bit of a sourpuss," as Abby put it—it seemed so petty in light of what she'd just heard. She knew, just by the way he forced the words out, that he'd told almost no one. Jeannie was familiar with that impulse, too. Half of her wanted to tell the whole world when Henry had died, to make the whole world pay attention and mourn with her, but another half of her wanted to run someplace where no one knew. Where she could pretend to be normal and whole and enjoy the lie.

He swiped his gaze away, sensing the exposure she felt so keenly, but his eyes were drawn back to the huge connection they unwillingly shared. Jeannie felt her pulse pound in her ears, felt the air scrape hard into her lungs. How had she ever thought him ordinary before?

"Nine years," he said, answering the question she hadn't yet asked. She heard the near decade of loneliness scorch the edges of his voice and burn in her own chest as well.

Chad kept his attention on the last box, eventually snapping the final battery into place and then lining all the smoke detectors up on the table. "I can test these for you, but I don't think that will really solve your problem."

"Why?"

"Because its not really smoke you're afraid of." He pulled a book of matches out of his pocket and Jeannie fought the urge to flinch.

"I remember hating the minister for even lighting a candle at my fiancée's memorial service."

Her throat worked in a gulp. "Why use matches? You said you didn't need them to test the smoke detectors."

"I don't," he said gently, "but you need them to test yourself. Jeannie, you need to get over this. You need to light a match."

Chapter Seven

"Oh, no, I'm not!" Jeannie blurted out her refusal, even though she was embarrassed Chad guessed her fear of flame. Did he have to strike such a nerve?

"Don't feel bad—I've seen sillier reactions on much more serious people. I can help. And I won't tell anyone."

Why would Chad Owens do something like this for her? Jeannie couldn't bring herself to ask the question. She just tried to think of a way out of this as Chad calmly put the matches on the table in front of her. Before she could come up with any refusal that didn't sound just plain chicken, he picked up the first detector and popped the top off the can. Jeannie clutched the windowsill. *It's worth a try.* He sprayed the substance into the detector, letting the alarm's screech fill the hollow space for a few seconds before he hit the device's reset button. "This one works."

"Yep." Jeannie gulped the single syllable out, still clutching the windowsill.

"And you're still here, still in one piece."

"Sort of." She tried to smile but it clearly didn't fool him. She really didn't want to start lighting matches with anyone, much less Chad Owens.

"So," he said in a voice that sounded too much like he knew what she was thinking, "step one is that you come over and just hold the box of matches while I test the next detector."

Jeannie's fear suddenly combined with a keen awareness of the space between them. "Do I have to?" She bit her lip. He picked the worst time to smile. "I do, don't I?"

"I'm a professional." He held out the box.

Slowly, carefully, cheering herself on again as she did while crossing the street, Jeannie rose and came around to his side of the table. Now she was aware of every inch between them. She couldn't hide her flinch when she took the box from him. "Nothing but hold it. That's all for this one."

He sprayed the can in front of the detector, which went off just as the first one did. The loud sound was oddly relieving, as if it startled the tension out of the room. "See? One step at a time. Next detector, I'll light the match you hand me."

Jeannie shook, but she did it. With every detector and its accompanying match task, her pulse came down. With the next detector, Chad had her blow out the lit match, and she surprised herself by laughing.

Jeannie felt her pulse go back up for entirely different reasons when Chad put down the can and said, "Come here and hold the box with me." They'd have to touch to hold the small box at the same time. His hands were big and warm, next to her pale hands that actually shook so much he had to place his hand on top of hers to keep the box steady.

"You can do this," he said in a tender voice. "You need to do this." He struck the match, and Jeannie realized her flinch wasn't nearly as powerful as before.

"That wasn't so bad," she offered, even though her voice wobbled. "On to the next one."

"Okay, but now we're in the big leagues.

I'll help." He tested the next detector without his eyes ever leaving hers. He'd managed to take this horrible hurdle and turn it into a game, a duel of dares that made her heart thump in her ears. As if helping her to strike that match was the most important thing he could do.

Once the detector silenced, Chad came around behind her, and Jeannie reeled with the knowledge of how close they were to each other. His arms reached easily around her small frame. His hand lingered the slightest bit on hers as he helped her hold the box and one match. "One, two…"

"Three." She thrust the matchstick against the box. It popped out of both their hands to land unlit on the floor. They nearly bumped shoulders as they both bent to retrieve it, and for a second he was so close she could smell the slight spice of the soap he used. It struck her as clean and charismatic; memorable but nothing fancy. "Another try," she said, looking up at him. When was the last time she felt anything this close to butterflies in her stomach? She'd had years of fear knotting her chest, but this was altogether different—a long-forgotten sensation now awake and stirring.

She hadn't meant to fall back against his chest when they lit the match. His hand wrapped around hers, and she heard his breath catch as together they stared transfixed at the tiny flame. She felt every single place he touched her, a flurry of tingles she wasn't ready to admit.

He blew out the match well before the flame had any chance to reach her fingers. "Your turn, solo." His voice was just the tiniest bit unsteady, but the power of his smile surprised her when she accepted the box from him to strike the final match on her own. He clapped—actually clapped—when she struck the match, and an idea burst into her mind. She knew he'd find it silly, childish even, but she simply couldn't resist.

Chad looked truly baffled when she began digging in her purse, but his mouth dropped plum open when she produced her box of birthday candles.

"You keep *birthday candles* in your handbag?"

"You never know when you'll need to celebrate. I'd clean forgotten these were in there." She had, until just now. "I've thrown out every candle—not that any survived... but well, my handbag's one of the few things that made it intact through the…" She skirted around the word *fire*. She fished one of the yellow striped candles and presented it to him. "I haven't got a cake, so we'll just have to wing it."

Chad raised an eyebrow as if cake and birthday candles were the oddest thing he'd ever heard of, but there was a smile hiding behind his eyes. "And we're lighting a candle because…"

"Because now I need to light a match to something happy, that's why."

The smile found its way to the surface, warm and encouraging—if a bit embarrassed—as Chad stood there with a yellow birthday candle in his fingers while Jeannie struck her first happy match.

Abby stopped her forkful of Belgian waffle midair. "This is Chad Owens you're talking about? The fire marshal Chad Owens, not some new, nicer Chad Owens who just moved into town?" Jeannie had just spilled the entire story over breakfast. She'd tried not to. Abby was the kind of insatiable matchmaker who would jump on this sort of thing. Jeannie made it halfway through breakfast without any mention of it, but

Abby had brought it up. Her craft store was right next to the hardware store, and evidently Ed had "shared" news of her purchases.

Jeannie supposed the revelation was inevitable. She'd been preoccupied all week with those smoke detectors; how Chad had helped her test them, how grateful she was to him for squelching her fear of flame when nothing else and no one else had been able to do so. He'd even stayed and helped her hang all of the devices. He'd been *nice*. More than nice, actually; he'd been charming.

"Canned smoke?" Abby arched an eyebrow. "Well, I suppose it makes sense. What does it say about a man when he brings you a can of smoke?"

Jeannie grimaced. "It says he wants to test your smoke detectors."

"That's all?"

This was exactly why Jeanne left out the part about the birthday candle. Not only did it seem silly, but it felt like a secret between them. She didn't dare tell Abby what Chad Owens' eyes did to her insides as she struck that final match without any help. God granted her a glimpse of the man Chad had been before the sad story he barely hinted at, the story she now knew gave him his "sour" nature.

She knew too much now. She knew the "sourpuss" everyone saw wasn't Chad's original true nature. She'd spied the lost layer of warmth behind his usual demeanor. It didn't seem logical that the two of them could affect each other so…deeply. It'd been a full two days and Jeannie still had no idea what to do with any of what she'd seen and felt.

She chose a cautiously neutral reply. "Evidently our Mr. Owens is full of surprises."

Abby peered at her and chewed thoughtfully. Then she started pulling at a blond curl, the way she did when she was planning something. Jeannie could virtually hear gears turning in the woman's head. "He's got his eye on you. You know what they say about 'where there's smoke'…"

"Oh, please, Abby, stop." Best to halt this here and now. Jeannie hadn't been as neutral as she thought, and that could only spell trouble.

"Why?" Abby asked. "*You've* already started."

This was why Jeannie should never have started talking about it at all. Why she considered canceling their weekly post-church-service breakfast. Abby was relentless—and entirely too accurate—about these sorts of things. "Now you know why Nicky says we'll need to move out of town if he ever got a girlfriend because 'Aunt Abby will go nuts.'"

"If? Not when?"

"Let's just say I'm not ready to consider the prospect of Nicky having a girlfriend."

"Ever?"

"Well, maybe when he turns twenty-five. I want grandchildren eventually, just not this decade."

"And you're trying to change the subject on me. We were talking about you. You and Chad Owens, specifically. Don't try to deny there's something there. It's all over your face and you're the worst liar I know."

She gave Abby her best glare. "I'll admit, he surprised me. He's much kinder than he lets on, and he's been great to Nicky. But *that's all.*"

Abby put down her fork and blew a curl out of her eyes. "Please. That's the farthest thing from 'all' I've seen all year. Why are you hiding it, resisting it like it's something bad? It could be something good. Really good." She picked up her fork again, spearing her waffle with conspiratorial glee. "You know, I'd written him off as too sulky for the likes of you, but I guess I was wrong." She narrowed her eyes, leaning forward with both elbows on the table. "Don't see him in church, though, so we might have to work on that."

"Abby…"

"Now *you* stop it. I refuse to sit there and let my best friend stay miserable. And you are. You paste a big smile over it, but you are. After all you've been through, what's so wrong about a little happiness?"

Jeannie took a breath to refute it all, but Abby held up a silencing finger. Her voice grew tender. "Frank and I loved Henry, we really did, but you and Nicky have been alone a long time. Maybe it's time to rebuild more than the store."

"Look, even if I was interested…"

"Will you cut this out? You *are*," Abby corrected relentlessly.

Jeannie put her hands up. "Even if I was a tiny bit interested…"

"Not so tiny…"

"…this is *absolutely* not the time," Jeannie cut her off. "There's too much going on. I'm pulled in a dozen different directions right now. My attention needs to be on getting Sweet Treats open as fast as possible so that Nicky and I can feel like we have our lives back."

That shut Abby up for all of ten seconds. She didn't even make it through buttering her toast before her next words bubbled up out of her. "You ever think he might be able to help you with that?"

"Help? We're talking about the man who has asked to see three different sets of plans on the store already. I don't need a watchdog looking over my shoulder."

Jeannie reached into her handbag for her wallet and spied the box of birthday candles still in there. She flushed, remembering how Chad had helped her light the match. Her skin tingled at the memory of his hand on hers.

"Whoa. You want to tell me what that was all about?"

"What?" Jeannie panicked. Had she been that obvious?

"That look you just got. Something did happen. Something so *something* you weren't even going to tell me about it."

Jeannie's only hope was to try and tell the facts without sending Abby into full-blown

Cupid mode. "He helped me light a match. I've been…afraid to lately. It's silly, really. He walked me through it, and, well, I suppose there was something there when he touched me."

Abby's eyes grew wide.

"See?" Jeannie pointed at her friend. "That's exactly why I didn't tell you. I knew you'd get like this."

"Like what? Happy? For my best friend? The horror!" Abby began cutting up her waffle, humming along with the country music playing in the restaurant. She had the look of someone who had just latched onto a wonderful plan and was already dreaming up ways to get started.

"I know that look, Abby. That look sent me to two pathetic 'older singles' Bible studies and on those awful dates with Frank's boring accountant colleagues." That look also announced a target had been acquired by one of nature's unstoppable forces.

"You want to know what I think?"

No, she didn't, but Jeannie knew it wasn't really a question. She steeled herself, took a sip of her coffee and prayed for grace.

"I think you've forgotten the difference

between a watchdog and someone to watch over you."

Why was Abby so good at saying exactly the thing to get under her defenses? Jeannie thought about Chad, and the way he'd pulled her out of the street in front of the firehouse. Somehow he'd taken command but not taken over. "Okay, maybe his attention really is genuine concern, and not authority. And yes, something is there." There was, and it was frighteningly strong.

"And then there is his connection with Nicky. He was right, wasn't he, about stopping you from rushing over to the school?"

"All right, yes," Jeannie admitted. "It would have made things worse if I'd rushed over there. Nicky made it quite clear he would have 'died of embarrassment' if I'd showed up."

"So, he's a good man. Hard to find these days."

"But he's so sad. There were good reasons not to get involved with a guy like that. All that unresolved dark side. Don't you think I've got enough of my own baggage to worry about without adding a brooding fire marshal?" It was a pathetic barrier but it was the best she could come up with in her confusion.

The Abby Reed Force of Nature smiled back at her. Abby swirled a bit of waffle into a puddle of syrup with a gesture entirely too close to a victory lap. "Only one way to find out. And you *want* to find out. You're just not quite ready to admit it yet."

That was so close to the truth that Jeannie choked on her reply. Thankfully, Abby backed off after that, moving on to other topics like Thanksgiving plans and the endless exploits of Abby's high-school senior son. Jeannie hoped the matter had been put to rest, if only temporarily, but as they were paying their bill Abby winked and asked, "So, when are you going to ask him to church?"

"Who?"

"You know very well who. When are you going to ask Chad Owens to church?"

Jeannie slipped her change into her yellow patent-leather wallet with a forced apathy. "I have no plans to ask Chad Owens to church. You're chair of the outreach committee, so why don't *you* ask Chad Owens to church?"

Not that Jeannie really thought that would end it, but Abby did take her outreach committee tasks of "head inviter" very seriously. There were very few folks in Gordon Falls Abby hadn't cajoled, invited or outright dragged into a church service. "Because," she said with a too-wide smile, "I'll be busy asking him to dinner Saturday night."

Jeannie balked. "But that's when Nicky and I are coming to dinner..." She didn't even get to the end of the sentence.

And so it began.

Somewhere in between the last smoke detector and the first match, Jeannie knew there was never any hope of stopping it in the first place.

Poor Chad. He'd never know what hit him.

Chapter Eight

This year's box had arrived.

Chad looked at it, running his fingers across the Chinese characters that covered the outside of the package. Laurie's mother was Chinese—Laurie's middle name had been Li-Fen—and sent one of these every year around the anniversary of Laurie's death. Her family had always managed a harmonious mix of Chinese and American cultures, as Laurie's dad, Tony, had been a missionary in China when the couple met. Laurie's mother, Huifen, or "Helen" as she called herself in the States, showed up on Chad's doorstep one fall day with the initial box.

"These are Chinese sky lanterns," she had declared in her clipped speech, holding up what looked like a yellow paper balloon. "In

China they are used at a festival in February, but we will use them now to remember Laurie." Laurie's family grafted a host of Chinese traditions into their strong Christian beliefs—"hybrids" Laurie had called them in her botanical nomenclature.

"Helen," he'd replied, "thanks for thinking of me, but please, I don't need this. I don't want this."

"You are young and grieving. How do you know what you need?" She had ignored his protests and deposited the box on his kitchen table. "These lanterns symbolize how our prayers send wishes to Heaven. They suit you. Centuries of Chinese have used lanterns to signal a return to safety."

Chad supposed it wasn't a bad impulse—Laurie probably would have loved it—but he didn't find the idea comforting in the slightest. He found it overblown and theatrical, but didn't say that out of respect for the woman who would have been his mother-in-law. She'd left the box with him, and Chad thought that would be the end of it.

Until Helen returned the next year with another box. "You need closure. This will give you closure," she'd proclaimed despite Chad refusing her as kindly as he knew how.

"I am not the kind of man who's going to find closure lighting paper lanterns and sending them up into the sky."

Helen had only smiled and continued her annual campaign, sending a box every fall since.

She hadn't succeeded. The arrival of Helen's box never signaled safety; it only marked the beginning of his cold sadness, the start of grappling his way through another holiday season alone.

Chad put the box into his truck, thinking maybe this year he'd bring it to the firehouse and find someone who'd enjoy the lanterns rather than stack them up with the other seven boxes in his garage. No sense letting something Helen had ordered all the way from China go to waste. Now that he thought of it, the whole charade reminded him of Jeannie's thing with the birthday candle— maybe *she'd* find a use for the lanterns.

Jeannie was finding her way into his thoughts constantly. He didn't know what to do with that, or what to do with the way his mind kept pulling back to the look in her eyes when she finally lit that silly candle. Something so ridiculous shouldn't have been nearly so satisfying, but he'd felt downright victorious when she'd blown the candle out. As if he'd managed to restore something important for her. He didn't know what to do with that, either.

He surprised himself when he went back into the house by doing something he hadn't done in years. Chad went to his closet and pulled down an aged manilla envelope. The paper was growing crisp and yellowing with time. Unwinding the red string closure, he could barely read the penciled October date in the upper right-hand corner. It was the only thing identifying the package. A date was all he could manage at the time. He couldn't even bear to write her name on it. It wasn't as if anyone else needed to be able to find it, and he'd never forget what it was or why it stayed on the top shelf of his closet.

The first page to slide out was the insurance company's "Incident Report." He'd always found that title insulting. "Incidents" were things like tripping over a curb or bumping someone's fender in the grocery store parking lot. This was a tragedy. That had been the word he used to describe the fire that took Laurie's life, and not for dramatic purposes. The day after the funeral, it had come to him from out of his memory.

"Oedipus Rex," his high school English teacher had said, "is a true tragedy."

"Are there false ones?" Chad had asked, more to mouth off than out of genuine curiosity.

"There are sad stories," the teacher had continued, "but they are not tragedies. Something tremendously sad becomes a tragedy when it doesn't have to happen."

Laurie's death didn't have to happen.

Chad felt like that condemnation had been scratched into his chest with a dull knife over and over for years. How many times had he chided Laurie for always climbing where she shouldn't in search of this plant and that? Laurie dove into nature—into *life*—with an abandon that made him crazy. If he'd ever thought she'd meet an early end, it would be falling from a tree or slipping down a cliff— something heroic out in nature's glory.

A space heater and branches of dried oak were neither dramatic nor glorious. They were stupid, preventable and ridiculously mundane. "Dried botanical specimens" were essentially kindling. What haunted Chad some nights when he couldn't sleep was how many times he'd thought to check the batteries in Laurie's smoke alarms but never *ac-*

tually done it. He hadn't even known she'd been taking sleeping pills—she'd been nervous about the wedding plans but never told him it had kept her awake at night.

On good nights he could console himself that she died in her sleep, peaceful and dreaming of the bright future they planned together. On the bad nights, he imagined her scrambling and coughing, flailing for a doorway too hidden by thick black smoke. Calling out his name to come and save her. George's son, Clark, one of Chad's closest friends at the time, had been the one to identify her engagement ring still on her charred finger. The coroner had refused to let him view the body, saying it would be too difficult an image to carry for the rest of his life.

He didn't see how it could be any worse than the visions he saw in the dark.

Laurie's engagement ring, still in the plastic bag from the funeral home, slid out of the envelope to ping softly on the table. Tony had a grieving father's tears in his eyes when he gave it back to Chad.

"I don't want it. It belongs on Laurie's finger."

"We chose to cremate her," Tony said. His face had aged decades in the few days since his daughter's death. "We thought we'd spread her ashes at the botanical garden. It suits her, surely you can see that. Take the ring, Chad. It should be yours."

Chad could never bring himself to take the ring out of the plastic bag, to touch something that had touched her for so long, for some irrational fear he'd wipe away her essence with his guilty fingertips.

He should have been able to do something. Anything. How many times had he seen the clutter of her cottage and convinced himself it was her vitality, her creativity spilling out everywhere? How many times had he swallowed this warning or that, unable to endure the disappointed look her carefree spirit would give him. "Oh, you," she would always say when he suggested wiser courses of action for this or that. And then she would shrug her delicate shoulders, give him a tender smile and kiss his forehead or something romantic like that. Seconds later—or sometimes many kisses later—she would be fluttering off to her next creative venture, leaving him to catch up. If God had ever really made wood nymphs, Laurie would have been one.

God. Now there was a thought he'd not

held in years. Laurie believed death led to a better place. She'd seen God's glory splashed all over nature, to hear her describe the world around her. Her parents had rock-solid faith, and they'd raised her to see God in everything and everyone.

Jeannie Nelworth was like that. In all the chaos that engulfed her, she never acted like God had turned His back on her. She'd lost even more than Chad had—widowed before thirty seemed especially cruel, and yet kept her faith and perhaps even deepened it. Whatever faith Chad possessed had left him when Laurie did, as if the faith had never really been his, only borrowed from Laurie and yanked back when she died. Jeannie had that infectious zest for life that had drawn him to Laurie.

A birthday candle. The woman kept birthday candles in her handbag, for crying out loud, as if life could serve up a surprise celebration at any moment. Had he even celebrated his last birthday?

What had he overheard Abby Reed calling him? A "sourpuss"?

He looked at their engagement photograph, pained to see a rugged, hopeful, younger version of himself with his arm firmly around Laurie. That man was no sourpuss.

"You are now," Laurie's almond eyes said to him from the photograph. It seemed so real that he actually shivered. "Don't be," she would have said, then touched his hair and wandered off.

Jeannie had touched his arm just as gently, and it had blasted through him, startling as it was soft. She must have known.

He collected the items back into their envelope. Before he even thought about what it meant, he took the yellow sparkly pen off his desk and wrote "Laurie's things" on the envelope. Gave it a name instead of a cold, clinical date. Laurie would probably have liked that some of the sparkle came off onto the envelope. And for the first time, Chad didn't hold his breath as he slid it back into its protected corner of his closet.

Jeannie nearly dropped the phone. "He *what?*"

"I know." Mrs. Hunnington thankfully sounded as shocked as Jeannie felt. Jeannie was not in the habit of getting calls from the school principal. "It's not like Nicholas to get into that big of a fight."

Jeannie sat down at her wobbly, borrowed kitchenette table, still in her pajamas. She looked at the oven clock—so old the clock still had hands, not digits—because she'd been cleaning all morning and hadn't even put on her watch. It was nine forty-five. Nicky had been in school for what? Two hours?

Something in Mrs. Hunnington's words caught her attention. "What do you mean 'that big of a fight'? Has he been in fights before?"

Mrs. Hunnington's sigh said too much. "Not really. Scuffles are a part of boys' lives at this age. There are days where we rival Animal Planet over here, so normally we don't call parents unless there's a point of concern."

A point of concern? Jeannie popped back off the ripped vinyl chair to head into her bedroom. "I find *any* fight of Nicky's concerning." She pulled open the flimsy folding panels of her closet door to rummage through the laundry for the jeans she'd worn yesterday. "You know everything he's been through," she defended as she started yanking them on. "I'll be right there."

"Actually," Mrs. Hunnington began. Her

hesitant tone made Jeannie pause. "I'd call Mark Billings before you come over."

Mark Billings? The dentist? Jeannie let the pant leg fall loose around her calf. "Why?" She didn't really need to ask.

"Well, it seems Nicholas got a tooth knocked loose."

The thought of anyone knocking into her boy hard enough to dislodge a tooth launched Jeannie into a protective mother's rage. "What on earth happened over there?"

"The other fellow has a serious black eye, so we're still working out who started it and why. They're both banged up."

"Nicky *gave someone a black eye?*" Jeannie was yanking her pants on so fiercely now it was a wonder they didn't come up to her chin. The Nicky she raised did not haul off and sock people. "I'll call Mark from the car on the way over."

"And…I'm sorry to say this, Jeannie, really I am, but I've had to suspend both boys for two days. It's board policy and blows were thrown on both sides so I don't have any choice. And in all honestly, I think they need to cool down and take their mistakes seriously. If Chad Owens hadn't been here to pull those two off each other, I'm not sure how far things would have gone."

Suspended! Nicky! Jeannie was doing the last button on the first shirt she could find. "Chad?"

"The fight broke out during an assembly on fire safety. We have one every year after we do the fire drill. It's the reason I didn't call you right away—I wanted to see if given the circumstances there was any way we could make an exception." She let out another sigh. "My hands are tied. Truly, I never expected something like this from Nicholas."

"Neither did I. I'll be there in ten minutes. Mrs. Hunnington, I'm so sorry for all this." Jeannie hung up the phone with her heart stuck in her throat. Yes, Nicky had been grumpy since the fire drill, but from what she heard from other moms, grumpy was standard operating mode for thirteen-year-old boys.

I've failed him, she thought as she shoved her feet into a pair of tennis shoes. Her worst fears had been realized: she hadn't moved fast enough. She looked around the depressing little bedroom, with its mismatched collection of borrowed furniture and its old curtains, knowing Nicky's room was even gloomier despite the four posters she'd hung. All this temporary housing, the coming holidays in this sterile apartment with all their old decorations lost—it was too much for someone of Nicky's age.

She could muster all her optimism of a better future soon but things right now weren't good. Not for Nicky. Not even for her. Abby was right—she'd merely plastered a smile over their misery. *He's only thirteen, Lord,* Jeannie pleaded toward Heaven and she fumbled with the car ignition. *You've asked so much of him already. We need to be in our new home, replanting his life instead of living out of boxes. I need that as much as he does. You have to know this. You have to want this for us, don't You?*

Jeannie had beaten down two bursts of tearful frustration by the time she reached the school parking lot. Henry's words came flooding into her memory, the calm way he'd taken charge during Nicky's first fever as an infant. "Be the parent, be the one who knows it'll all be okay," Henry had always said. As if "okay" were as simple as declaring "it'll all be okay." Somehow, Henry always managed it. During the chicken pox, strep throat, that time Nicky broke his thumb into such a gruesome shape Jeannie almost fainted looking at it, Henry held steady and made it all okay.

Now she had to hold steady. She had to walk into that school knowing things would work out, certain of Nicky's future despite this bump—this *big* bump—in the road. Jeannie had to walk into Mrs. Hunnington's office as a parent who knew her son's true nature. She had to be the one making sure everyone knew Nicky wasn't sliding down some slippery slope to juvenile delinquency.

"He's not," Jeannie repeated into the rearview mirror until she could say it confidently. "He's not a bad kid. He's just made one bad choice." She'd read that phrase in one of the two dozen parenting books that used to sit in her living room. Before the books—and everything else—had burned. *Don't go there.* "Stop," she commanded the Jeannie in the rearview mirror. "Be the parent. Be Mom in Control."

Oh, God, You're going to have to help me because I don't feel one bit of Mom in Control.

Jeannie took in a deep breath, repeating the single word that had pulled her through the worst of life after the fire. Grace. Grace.

"My grace is sufficient for you," scripture said. Nicky needed grace. Grace would pull them from this tangle. He'd made an error— a serious error—but grace would lead him home. He'd lost control, which was exactly why she couldn't. She steeled herself as Nicky's Protector and Agent of Grace and walked toward the school's big, red doors.

Red, Lord? Was that really necessary?

Chapter Nine

Nicky looked worse than she felt. He was slumped sideways on an olive vinyl couch in the nurse's office, a stuffed backpack on the floor beside him. He banged his foot against a gray metal side table as if bored. His royal blue shirt—one of only two to survive the fire—now sported a torn sleeve and an unsettling blood stain on the neck. A good-size bruise bloomed on his jawbone, just below the bloody ice-stuffed towel he currently held to his mouth.

Mrs. Hunnington was right, this had been no mere scuffle. Jeannie swallowed the impulse to rush up and assess his considerable wounds and now-ruined shirt. The surge of anger and embarrassment she felt helped keep such a gush of sympathy in check.

She stood there, wordless, waiting far too long for Nicky to look up at her with narrowed, unreadable eyes. Anger, pain, guilt and confusion all vied in his gaze. It was times like these where Jeannie felt Henry's absence stab her in the chest like a physical knife.

She set her handbag down with forced calm. "You want to tell me what this is all about?"

"How about I fill you in?" Chad Owens' voice came from the doorway behind her.

"How about I hear from *my son first?*" she shot back, suddenly annoyed. Somewhere between the apartment and school, Chad had become part of the problem instead of part of the solution. Something in the presentation must have set the two boys off. Where was the care Chad promised to take on these subjects? Why was she the only person who remembered this boy had just lost everything he had to a fire?

Chad stepped farther into the room but kept his hand on the doorknob. "He needs to keep icing that lip, and I *really* think I ought to talk to you first." He tone was nearly a command, and to back it up he pushed open the door and gestured out into the hallway.

Chad Owens had a lot of nerve. Nicky, of course, took that cue to look as if he'd feel infinitely better if she left the room. Torn, she darted her gaze back and forth between the two glaring males and settled for a look she hoped broadcast "I'm not done with you yet" loud and clear to Nicky before following Chad out into the hallway.

"It's not his fault," Chad said the minute the door clicked behind him. "You need to know that. The other kid, Scott Collins, laid into Nick about his nervousness during the fire drill. Let's just say Scott wasn't exactly kind. I'm not defending Nick's punch, but I can't say I wouldn't have thrown one myself under the circumstances."

Now she knew why Mrs. Hunnington hadn't mentioned the other boy involved over the phone—it would have sent her into a panic. Scott Collins was huge and mean. One of those massive eighth-graders who looked like he'd be shaving tomorrow and wiped sixth-graders off the bottom of his sneakers each night.

"Nicky punched *him?*" Only something really mean would get that big a rise out of Nicky. "What did Scott say?"

Chad shook his head. "Nothing I care to repeat and nothing you'd want to hear. According to the nearest teacher, the words 'pyro' and 'fire-freak' were used. Along with a lot of other choice words that earn you an instant detention."

Jeannie leaned against the wall. The cold ceramic tile matched the chill down her spine. They had to be talking about some other boy, not her son. Even on his worst days, this didn't sound like Nicky. "Nicky cussed?"

Chad wiped his hands down his face, while a bell rang down some distant noisy hallway. "No," he said, clearly upset, "Scott did all the cussing." She'd jumped to the wrong conclusion; he did feel some responsibility in the situation. "He shoved Nick, and Nick fell into the corner of the gym riser."

So it was the gym riser that took out Nicky's tooth. That shouldn't have made it any better, but it did, somehow. Less malicious, more accidental.

"Nick told Scott to back off," Chad went on. "Not nicely, I'm afraid, and with a couple of shoves of his own. Obviously, Scott didn't. All this was going on while I was taking a fire extinguisher out of a box for a demonstration. Then the fire alarm went off because one of Scott's buddies pulled it, and well, things escalated from there."

It sounded like a mob scene, with her son as the target. Control went out the window. "They pulled a fire alarm on a fight over a fire alarm? They ganged up on him like that?"

Chad put his hands out, trying to calm her down. "Hang on, we don't know any of that for sure. A lot went wrong all at once. I just thought you ought to know Nick was definitely provoked. Still, a punch is a punch, and hits were thrown on all sides. I expect it'll take a few days to sort out."

"A few days of *suspension,*" Jeannie shot back, feeling entirely too cornered.

"Zero tolerance is exactly that." When she gave him a look, he added, "And 'provoked' is not the same as 'innocent.'"

"I know that." Jeannie failed to keep the edge out of her voice. She pushed off the wall, her pacing steps echoing off the rows of metal lockers.

"And Jeannie, you should know..."

"Just a minute, Mr. Collins." Mrs. Hunnington was stepping outside her office a few feet away. She closed the door behind her and walked over to Chad and Jeannie. Her expression grew a black hole in Jeannie's stomach. "You were able to reach Dr. Billings?"

"Yes. Nicky has an appointment in fifteen minutes." Jeannie checked the watch she'd managed to put on before leaving the house. "Mrs. Hunnington, *how* did this happen?"

"I'm working on that, but Jeannie..." Chad's expression darkened even more, and the look that passed between him and the principal told Jeannie that for the third time this morning, things were about to go from bad to worse.

Mrs. Hunnington took off her glasses and put a terribly serious hand on Jeannie's shoulder. "Jeannie, I'm sorry to have to tell you that we found two lighters in Nicholas's locker. And a half-empty box of matches."

Chad stared at Jeannie as she walked down the building with one arm clamped around Nick. She looked like someone shot a cannon through her chest when Mrs. Hunnington told her about the matches. As if every ounce of sunlight left her eyes in the same second. Had her emotions always displayed so transparently in her eyes, or had he just become attuned to them? He turned to the principal, his own niggling suspicion reflected in the woman's concerned eyes. She'd stopped just short of saying what he was already thinking; Nicky was likely setting fires. "He's in more trouble than we thought."

She sighed. "I'm worried Jeannie can't see it, or won't see it. It'd be far too easy to shift all the blame to Scott here."

Chad could almost be proud of Nick for standing up to the brute. "There's more than enough to go around. Scott is nearly twice Nick's size and the mouth on that kid shocks me. He egged Nick on because he's a bully."

"I have as much empathy for the underdog as any parent, but Chad, even you can see the fighting was only the symptom here, not the problem." The principal put her glasses back on and gave out a weary sigh.

"I know, I know. Nick Nelworth is a slow-boiling pot of something—guilt, anger, resentment, all of the above. That punch was just the steam escaping for the first time."

And maybe not the first time—half the matches were gone. Chad nodded toward the door where Jeannie and Nick had left. "Really, who could fault the kid? He's all of thirteen and grappling with everything life has thrown at him. Of course he'd come up short."

She planted her hands on her hips, every inch the schoolmaster. "As much as it hurts me, yes, I *can* blame him. It can't be tolerated. He needs help."

Chad's heart seemed to lurch out the door behind the boy, aching with the certainty Nick needed help but unsure how to convince Jeannie to get it for him. "The county does have a program, but I don't know that we need to go that far yet."

"Why? A fire survivors program might do him a world of good."

"It's a fire starters program."

"Then I'd say the ball's in your court, Chad. I'll have Mrs. Corning give you whatever information she can, but we don't actually know Nick is starting fires. I'll need you to help with that assessment. You can bring anyone from the county in on it you'd like, or you can handle it locally. Agreed?"

"Jeannie would never go for it. She'd think it labeling Nick as troubled, and she wouldn't be entirely wrong." Yet, how could Nick not be troubled? It seemed such an enormous problem. He was a full-grown man and knew how powerless *he* felt against an onslaught of tragedy. How could anyone teach a thirteen-year-old boy to handle it?

"It's not fair." He said it to Mrs. Hunnington, but in reality, Chad realized he was yelling at God. God? Now? After leaving his faith in the dust for all the years since Laurie's death, it seemed an unlikely time to try and restart the conversation. Over the years, he'd found a way to spit out all God had "done" to assail him, to reject the thought of God still being in control and resign himself to his sorry lot. That tactic no longer worked. Watching Jeannie's eyes and sensing the turmoil in Nick, Chad found he simply could no longer swallow the thought that the God who professed to love had allowed this to happen to Nick. Why, why would God put a boy through something so painful, allow such deep scars in someone so young?

"I'll take it from here." The pressing, inescapable truth was that Chad had seen this coming, but had brushed it off as the school counselor's job. It wasn't. It was his. The school counselor probably skimmed two dry textbook chapters on some post-traumatic studies. Chad had actually *lived* through a fire and its emotional aftermath. He'd recognized the scars on Nick, but talked himself out of getting involved, convinced himself he was making assumptions, and look what happened. Nick was most likely setting fires—or at the very least, thinking about setting fires. Chad had to step in before the boy did something more dangerous. He could no longer take the chance that Jeannie would be blinded by her insistence that things were okay.

As he left the school and drove by the yellow Jeep that sat outside Dr. Billings's office, Chad couldn't stop himself from parking his truck. He needed to apologize, to make sure Jeannie wasn't alone.

He walked into the office to find Jeannie perched alone on the edge of the waiting room couch, eyes shut, hands gripping a rolled-up magazine as if it were a life raft. Her mint-green shirt now bore a smudge of reddish-brown blood. She didn't even hear him come in. Why hadn't she called anyone to come help her through this? "Jeannie?"

Her eyes flew open. The fear and worry he saw so easily now—had they always been there? When had he lost the one-dimensional, too-sunny impression he'd once had of her? He saw now how she fought for her joy, tooth and nail. Clung to it the way she currently vise-gripped that magazine.

Her eyelashes were wet. He wasn't sure if the closed eyes he saw a moment ago meant she'd been praying, or simply trying not to cry. Either thought—or both—dissolved whatever resistance he still had left, and Chad walked over to put a hand on her shoulder. He felt useless at her anguish, knew he'd probably end up hurting her more, but couldn't possibly leave her alone.

A teardrop plopped down on the magazine cover. Even in the firehouse, she'd never succumbed to tears. It killed him to see it now. "Fights? Lighters and matches?" she nearly whispered, wiping her cheek with the back of one hand. He fished into his coat pocket and pulled out a tissue, a poor alternative to the crazy part of him that wanted to reach out and wipe that tear away.

"He's been through a lot." Chad groped

around for the right thing to say. "He's just bumping around in all of it, trying to find his way out. He's just got…too much going on inside." He tried to think of something Laurie's mother would say, reaching back into his catalogue of Helen's endless attempts to comfort him. "He's a good kid, you know that. Everyone knows that."

She blew her nose, a tiny little sound he found ridiculously endearing. "Scott Collins doesn't know that."

"If I were a less honorable man, I'd tell you how much I'd like to take Scott Collins out back behind the firehouse and teach him a lesson about kicking someone when they're down."

"You and I both know that's not the answer here."

That was true, but Chad's urge to seek revenge for Nick's beating wasn't interested in listening to reason. Life had beaten enough out of Nick—*nobody* got to add to that wound.

Mark Billings poked his head through the sliding half window that looked out into the waiting room. "He's going to be fine, Jeannie. Another twenty minutes or so. The swelling's already gone down considerably.

Oh, good, you're not alone," he said, nodding at Chad. "In another minute I was going to have the hygienist call Abby, you looked so bad." The window slid shut and Billings disappeared.

There was no way he could bring up any kind of program now. She was already sinking fast and she still had to get through this appointment and the drive home. "Look," Chad began even though he felt completely wrong at this, "it was a dumb choice, but maybe there's some good in the fact that Nick felt strong enough to stand up to the likes of Scott Collins. He didn't play victim here. The impulse was right, just the wrong methods." Maybe, if he could just start her off on her usual find-the-silver-lining plan, she'd recover enough strength to get through this part.

Jeannie looked up at him, so he ventured into trickier territory. "The fight's just anger getting out of control. It's the matches we really need to be worried about."

Bad move. She wasn't ready to hear that, and it showed all over her face. "What was he doing with matches in his locker? *Matches,* Chad. What's going on inside his head?"

It was as if she'd never said his name

before. Which was idiocy—they'd lived in the same town for years, served on two town committees, had dozens of conversations. Yet the plea in her voice cut loose something in his chest that felt like both calm and panic at the same time. Something that gave him the disastrous urge to pull her to his chest and let her sob buckets into his shirt.

"I don't know," he said, feeling absolutely helpless to bring her to the conclusion currently clawing at his brain. "We need time to figure it out." He'd used "we" again. He was involved, invested, determined to see this boy and his mother out of the valley he'd now have a hand in making. "We need to help him figure it out. Fire becomes something…different…to people who've survived it. Especially kids. They either run to it or run from it. You ran from it," he said, his mind racing back to the feelings he had watching her light that birthday candle, "maybe Nick's run *to* it." He was thinking out loud now, searching desperately for some other, less darker explanation that would suit her mindset. He couldn't abandon her to cold, hard facts—not only because they were cruel, but because he didn't have any yet. "Maybe he lit matches to prove to himself he wasn't afraid of fire. Or prove it to kids who were teasing him the same way you had to prove it to yourself with the matches. We're going to have to let him tell us what's going on inside his head."

"We?" It was a small, frail syllable. He was truly sunk: she'd noticed.

Chapter Ten

Jeannie sent Nicky straight to his room once they got to the apartment. He made it quite clear he wasn't in the mood for conversation, keeping his face away from her and slumping down in the car seat as they drove home, and Dr. Billings told him to keep the ice on his mouth another half an hour anyway.

Jeannie wasn't feeling talkative, either. She prayed for wisdom the whole drive home. Or just grace, perhaps, to keep from doing further damage until she could untangle her thoughts and emotions. The laundry lay half undone where she'd left it, and dishes sat in soapy water long gone cold. She hadn't had the chance to eat lunch, but she had no appetite anyhow.

One look at her kitchen calendar told her

there wasn't much time for quiet contemplation; she was due at a church committee meeting in an hour. "Not doing that." Jeannie sighed as she hit the speed dial button on her phone, thankful the committee chair was Abby. If Abby hadn't already heard—and news might have spread quickly enough that she had—maybe recounting things to a good friend would bring some clarity.

"I practically had my hand on the phone," Abby said when she picked up on the first ring. "I almost called you but I figured you'd call when you came up for air. Suspended for fighting. What a mess. I'm so sorry all this is happening."

"'Mess' is a good word." Jeannie picked Nicky's jacket up off the hallway floor where he'd dumped it, but once she noticed the bloodstain on the collar she tossed it toward the laundry pile still on the floor rather than the coatrack. Having to go downstairs to the apartment basement to do laundry was just another part of why she disliked living here. "I thought I could handle whatever Nicky threw at me, even on his worst days."

Abby sighed. "This is a bit more than your average teen parenting bump, isn't it?"

Jeannie couldn't decide whether to ask

Abby if she knew about the matches. Matches sounded so…criminal. This was no bump. This felt like a solid brick wall she had no idea how to climb. "Have I fooled myself, Abby?"

"What do you mean?"

"Was I wrong to think we'd come through this unscarred?" She leaned against the wall, feeling trapped in the narrow beige tunnel. Not one square inch of her new place would be beige if she could help it. "I kept being so thankful God granted us some kind of emotional immunity, had protected us so well through all this."

"You have. You've been amazing. People are inspired by how well you've handled things."

"But that's just it. I've been so busy looking for evidence of how well things were going that I didn't see signs that might have pointed to this."

"I don't think anyone could have been prepared for this." Abby's voice grew soft. "I would have come to help if you called. In a heartbeat. You know that, don't you?"

"I do. It's okay, Chad was there at Dr. Billings's office."

"Chad was there?"

Jeannie really hoped Abby had enough sense not to make anything of that right now. "He was giving a talk to the kids when the fight broke out." She still couldn't believe she had to use phrase "fight broke out" when discussing her son. "I'm not coming this afternoon."

"Of course not. You've got more important things to worry about than the Thanksgiving Food Drive. If you want, I'll tell Frank to make his own dinner and I'll come by after the meeting. If you need some time to talk."

"No," Jeannie surprised herself by answering. "I think I'd better start by talking to Nicky."

"Okay, but call me if you need me."

"Thanks."

Jeannie hung up the phone with the sad realization that she had no more clarity than before. Talking with Abby almost always made things better, but right now the knots in her life seemed to be far too big for any hope of assistance. She'd been blindsided by the entire day: Nicky getting into fights, suspension, matches and Chad. She pulled the stopper out of the sink drain.

Chad. Honestly, Jeannie didn't know if Chad's involvement made things better or worse. Did his offer of help simplify or complicate things? It had felt so good to have him there in the dentist's office. She was starting to feel a serious attraction to him, but she believed what she told Abby; this wasn't the time to add a relationship to her life. Today had proven she needed to focus on Nicky now more than ever.

She finished the dishes in the sink, hoping for a small sense of orderly accomplishment that never came. Taking a deep breath, Jeannie dried her hands and walked down the hallway to knock softly on Nicky's bedroom door. A grunt was her only reply. She pushed open the door to find Nicky sprawled on the corner of his bed, looking nothing like the sweet boy she knew. He'd abandoned the ice pack and was fiddling with a rubber band. At her entrance, he sat up, leaning back against the wall alongside his twin bed. He'd had a wonderful, big bed in their old place but already this borrowed twin bed looked too small for him. He avoided her eyes.

Jeannie sat down on the bed, moving the ice pack from its damp spot on the drab brown comforter. She wiped the last of the dishwater from her hands across the jeans she'd thrown on in her hurry. They had ketchup on them from last night when she and Nicky had laughed endlessly at one of his dumb jokes at the diner. That boy seemed a complete stranger to the one before her now. "You want to tell me what happened today?"

He let his head fall against the wall. "I'm sure Mrs. H. told you all about it."

"I want to hear it from you."

Nicky fidgeted, looked everywhere but at her for a long time, then said, "Scott Collins is a jerk."

Jeannie started to say "And we always punch jerks?" but she stopped herself, trying to think of what Henry or even Chad might say instead. "Why?" seemed the best choice.

"He thinks he owns the world. Like he's better than everyone, knows everything and the rest of us can just go… We don't stand a chance. How come everyone believes what he says even if it's stupid? I hate him."

His eyes flicked up to Jeannie, knowing she usually didn't like him to say he hated anyone. He looked like he hated Scott. Jeannie chose to let it slide, glad he had at least looked at her for the first time in an hour. She scooted herself back on the lower half of the bed, so that they both sat side by side at the head and foot of the bed, feet dangling over the side. For some reason, her brain chose that moment to notice his legs were not much shorter than hers now. How many years before he would tower over her, a lanky high school teen? "What could he say that would be stupid enough to make you hit him?"

Nicky dropped the rubber band and pulled his knees up, wrapping his arms around them and looking away from her. "Stuff," he said softly. He was still looking away from her, and she noticed he flexed the fingers of his right hand. His knuckles were still red from the punch.

She waited for him to offer up the details, but he didn't. He barely moved, just jiggled one foot nervously. She was going to have to pull it out of him, but it was going to have to be slow and gentle even though she wanted to take him and shake him to his senses. She shifted on the bed to face him. His shoulders seemed so broad and so small at the same time. "What'd he say, Nicky?"

"He said…" He stopped, and Jeannie raised her hand to put it on his shoulder, but something stopped her with her hand in midair. She waited, praying. The phone rang, but she let the machine pick it up, unwilling to move. "He said I was a freak. A pyro. Said I burned down my own house and that I should just go ahead and burn down the whole school. That I acted weird at the fire drill because I knew they were coming to get me. I hate him."

So much for one young man to take. How do kids learn to be so cruel? The pain in Nicky's voice sliced at her, making her want to lash out at anyone who would do something so awful as say "arson" to a kid whose house had just burned to the ground. Jeannie wondered for a second if she, too, wouldn't have punched Scott Collins if she were in Nicky's place. That wasn't a helpful sentiment.

"Mrs. Hunnington found matches in your locker."

No response.

It had to be asked. "You don't start fires, do you, Nicky?"

He whipped around at that. "What do you think?" he snarled out before getting up to sit in a chair on the opposite side of the room.

She pulled her legs up to sit cross-legged, exhaustion pressing down on her shoulders. "I don't know what to think. I know how I *thought* you behaved. But that boy doesn't punch people." She made herself hold his gaze, even though his eyes looked dark and foreign. "Tell me if what I know isn't true anymore."

"I know you're too scared to even light a match." His chin jutted out as he declared it. "I'm not. Yeah, I lit the matches. But I don't start fires. I didn't start *the* fire."

"No one thinks you did," she replied quickly, firmly. She didn't want Nicky believing Scott Collins's accusation for even a moment.

The look he gave her in reply sent a chill down her spine.

Chad kept looking at those ridiculous yellow sparkle pens every ten seconds, no matter what work he tried to do. Hoping distance would help, Chad started to drive home, but only got halfway before he pulled off the road and stared at his cell phone for a solid minute. *Don't do that. They need to be left alone to work this out for now. They need time.* He sighed and tossed the phone onto the passenger seat unopened, only to end in the parking space in front of Jeannie's apartment ten minutes later.

The lights were on inside. They were finally home and safe.

The thought of her in there grappling with Nick's issues all alone bothered him. He'd seen things in Nick no one else could see, and yet he'd failed to be there when Nick needed him. Twice.

He dialed the apartment phone number Nick had given him. *I'll just make sure they're okay, then go home.*

No one answered.

He lectured himself on the dangers of any further meddling the entire walk up to her door. He rang the bell even as he told himself what a bad idea it was. All of that evaporated in the look of relief that warmed Jeannie's face when she opened the door.

"You all okay?" he blurted out, thrown by how much her and Nick's pain had affected him. "You didn't answer your phone."

"I can't handle this." She leaned back against the doorway, clearly trying not to cry. She'd always been so feisty; this tearful delicacy had all but undone him. He'd let her into his world, let both of them in not because he wanted to, not because it was wise, but because he simply couldn't fight it anymore.

"Of course you can," he said. "You can

pull Nick through this, Jeannie, you can." It wasn't empty platitudes; he believed she could.

He looked down, realizing he'd grabbed her hand without meaning to. Her gaze traveled down to his hand on hers, then slowly back up to meet his eyes. A feathery lock of her hair fell from the messy ponytail she wore. His heart seemed to drop out of his chest altogether, leaving a hollow, precarious feeling that stole his breath. She knew. He could no longer pretend nothing had sprung up between them.

She clearly felt the same tug he did, that unending pull toward each other that had kept him up many nights and unhinged him for the last hour. Now what?

"Um…why don't you come in?" she asked, turning a shade of pink that tickled him somewhere inside. She started to turn. "Nicky's in his room. I think he's asleep."

"Jeannie…" he began, not even sure of what he ought to say.

"Please," she pleaded, and that was the end of it. He couldn't help but follow her up into the small, sparse apartment that looked nothing like any home Jeannie Nelworth would own. She'd tried to make the haphazard col-

lection of borrowed furnishings comfy, for
there was an afghan thrown over this or a
picture leaned up against that wall, but the
whole apartment felt keenly out of character
for her. He wasn't surprised when she blurted
out, "I hate this place. Nicky hates it, too.
Now can you see how badly we need to be
out of here? This is no home. It's not what
Nicky needs."

Jeannie had said so before, but here it was
palpable. He could see, now, what drove her
urgency. She walked into the tiny kitchen,
where she paced like an animal in pain. "He
told me he lit those matches. What am I supposed to do with that?"

He was glad Nicky admitted to at least
that. "Face it, I suppose. Get him help." He
hated what those words did to her eyes.

"I'm not strong enough to face this." Her
voice sounded thin and frail.

"You? You're the strongest woman I know.
You're not weak, Jeannie. You're just...
tired." She was weary. *I could be strong for
you,* he longed to say but knew that wasn't
a promise he could keep. She deserved so
much more than what he could give her. He
allowed himself to put one arm around her.
Not a hug, just one arm.

She looked up at him, and Chad recognized how dangerous it was for him to come here. His brain was already dreaming up lies he'd love to believe. She could be the woman who pulled him back to faith. Nothing short of her relentless buoyancy, her absolute unshakable faith could rekindle what was left of his. What if…?

A thump caught his attention, and he turned to find Nick standing in the kitchen doorway. He hadn't even changed his shirt, and the sight of the red bloodstain on his sleeve felt like a punch to Chad's stomach. The boy's red-rimmed eyes flicked from Chad to the hand Chad still had on Jeannie's shoulder. When his gaze came back to stare darkly at Chad, Nick's face looked at once too old and too young. "What are *you* doing here?"

Chapter Eleven

Jeannie couldn't say which was worse; the "gotcha" feeling in her stomach, or Nicky's searing gaze. She could easily explain that Nicky hadn't seen anything but an arm offered in comfort, but on the inside Jeannie knew her emotions went much further than her actions. Weary and frightened, she'd very nearly lost control of her feelings when Chad touched her. She knew, down deep, that had they been alone she might very well have kissed him. And that while he would have hesitated at first, he would have kissed her back. All of which was making it hard to think and breathe at the moment.

"I came to see if you and your mom were okay." Chad sounded casual, stable. How did men do that? Separate things and lay them aside as if life could be peeled into neat segments like an orange? Her thoughts were scattered and her breathing raced, but his voice held no hint of any emotional struggle.

"We're fine," Nicky barked, not looking at Chad. He headed for the fridge. "What's for dinner?"

Jeannie huffed and sat down. *What's for dinner?* As if it were a perfectly ordinary day. "I don't know. I haven't gotten that far." She tried not to make her glare sharp, but Nicky's subsequent eye roll told her she'd failed.

"Well, I'm hungry, that's all." He fished a gallon of milk out of the fridge, still acting as if Chad weren't in the room. "Can we get a pizza?"

"No, we cannot get a pizza. This is not a 'let's go get a pizza' kind of day, Nicholas."

"Fine," Nicky grumbled. "Whatever."

Jeannie kept her exasperation barely under control. She hadn't even thought about what she'd do with Nicky for the two days he was suspended. There were loads of work to do at the shop, she had set aside time in the church kitchen tomorrow to make several batches of candies for internet gift basket orders, but right now she and Nicky couldn't seem to be in the same room without arguing. "And just what exactly are you going to do tomorrow?"

Nicky sidestepped her and pulled a glass from the cabinet, pouring himself milk. "Stay home from school. I thought we all knew that."

Oh, how she hated that snippy tone of voice he could use. Harmless words but soaked in a nasty attitude. Half of her wanted to hug the poor wounded boy who was lashing out while the other half wanted to yell at the foolish young man who'd tried to solve things with his fists. "You did not earn yourself a day off here."

The idea came to her in a heartbeat. The firehouse might be the best place for him. Chad had a connection with the boy that went far beyond their mutual experiences of loss. She truly believed Chad could help Nicky sort out his feelings if they spent time together. "Chad, is there anything he can do down at the station? Chores or such?"

Nicky actually looked up. "Like for pay?"

She narrowed her eyes at her son. Did he really not grasp the seriousness of what happened today? "Absolutely not. I see this more like community service."

"You mean like a giant detention?" Nicky didn't share her optimism.

Chad, despite his look of surprise, didn't seem entirely unwilling. She'd sprung this imposition on him, but she didn't have loads of options and he'd clearly offered to help at the dentist's office. She raised her eyebrows at him, pleading for cooperation.

Chad ran a hand across his chin. She hoped he was cataloguing a list of unpleasant tasks for Nicky. "I think we could keep you busy, if you don't object to a little hard work."

So he *had* caught her intentions. This couldn't feel like a vacation—this suspension had to hurt. Hopefully a lot. The paperwork and swatch-wrangling at Sweet Treats just wouldn't fit the bill, and the last thing she needed was him underfoot while she cooked. It was hard enough to keep her own concentration, much less focus his. "I don't object one bit," she cut in before Nicky could reply. "The harder the better."

Nicky swallowed half the glass in two gulps, then refilled it and walked toward the door, leaving the gallon out on the counter. "Fine."

Her son's single, curt syllable stomped on

Jeannie's last nerve. "We are not done with this, Nicholas. Not by a long shot." She stood up from her chair. Nicky dragged himself back around to face her. "Put the milk away, thank Mr. Owens and then go start on that math Mrs. Hunnington sent home with you. I want it done before dinner, and then you and I have a long conversation ahead of us."

Nicky grunted something she hoped was "Thanks, Mr. Owens," deposited the milk in the refrigerator and left the room.

Jeannie let out her breath and sank wearily back down to the chair, letting her head fall into one hand braced on the table. "Am I awful for being relieved Nicky had somewhere else to go tomorrow?"

Chad shook his head. "No, actually, I think it's a very good idea. The smart plan of a woman with lots of fight left in her."

She hated how the threat of tears wound tight around her throat. "You're wrong. I have no plan at all and I don't have any fight left in me to keep this up. I'm on empty. Below empty. He's a mess. I'm a mess. God is going to have to step in and work some kind of miracle here."

"You believe in miracles, Jeannie."

"I believe in prayer. I can call Abby back

tonight, tell her the *whole* story and get people to pray."

"That sounds like you have more of a plan than you think."

"But then people would have to know all the details. The matches. They'll start looking at Nicky as a troubled boy. He's not. Scott Collins is wrong, Chad. Wrong. Nicky's not a…criminal. My son is not a pyromaniac—whatever that really means. He's just…better than this."

Chad's eyes widened. "Is that what Scott said to Nick? What started the fight?"

"Part of it. I can't get all of it out of him just yet. He's fighting me every step of the way." She could barely stand to look at Chad. "He used to tell me everything. Now…"

"He needs some help. Just a bit, just to get over a tough spot." The knot in her throat twisted tighter so that all she could do was look up at Chad and will herself not to cry. The regret in his eyes broke her heart.

"I don't know. I don't know anything for certain anymore." It sent a longing through her so strong it was like fighting a physical force urging her up out of the chair and into his arms. That was dangerous. She couldn't think clearly at all right now. She fingered the suspension papers lying on the kitchen table. "You should probably go."

"I'm sorry it's come to this. Really, I am. But it's here." He looked at her carefully. "We need to see it through. There are programs…"

"No. No programs. None of that teen offender stuff. Pyromania. That's not Nicky, and you know it." She pushed away the papers with flailing hands, feeling helpless. She hated to feel helpless, hated to think of Nicky as damaged. Troubled. Labeled. *Criminal.*

"You said yourself, we don't know what he hasn't told us." The pained uncertainty in his voice scared her to death.

"Maybe this is all there is. Maybe this is God's way of letting it out now before… before…"

"Before what? He's already suspended. Whatever's coming is already here."

"Well, whatever's here *can't have him.*" She wanted to crumple those papers and throw them against the wall. Still, Nicky's well-being was worth everything. Anything. "I'll just have to dig up the strength somewhere, won't I? Find some way to fight him out of this if it takes every blessed ounce I have to give." Jeannie squinted her eyes shut, wiping at the hot trickle that ran down her cheeks. "Only I don't feel like I *have* anything left to give." She kept her eyes shut, holding the world out of sight, feeling as if the chair was the only thing holding her upright.

A hand rested on Jeannie's shoulder, cautious and tender. Without opening her eyes, she gave in to the longing, and lifted one hand to rest atop his. A jolt shot through his fingers as she did so. His hands were strong against her shoulder. It seemed like centuries since a man had touched her in anything but friendship, and while this touch was full of compassion, there was more than friendship in it. It spoke clearly, if reluctantly, of other things.

She willed herself not to open her eyes; she knew what would happen if she did. She felt him, sensed him lean down toward her and her breath all but halted. If he touched her cheek, or did anything else tender like that, she'd be lost. "You should probably go." The words barely made it out of her throat.

After a long moment, she felt him pull back up.

"Bring him by tomorrow morning." She

opened her eyes to see him walking toward
the door. "I'll be there."

I'll be there. She grabbed those words and
clung to them like a lifeline.

"I think you like my mom."

Chad thought he'd finally gotten Nick
to the point where he'd discuss yesterday's
fight, but as conversation-halting statements
went, Nick had chosen wisely. He knew it,
too.

Not that Chad wasn't an easy target. Sleep-
lessness had sapped his energy, leaving
him without enough clarity to get through
the day with a surly, uncooperative Nick.
They'd done an hour of washing equipment
and small talk, but today wasn't just about
hard labor or killing time. He was supposed
to be helping Nick sort through the storm of
his emotions.

Chad pretended to search the kitchen for
coffee creamer while his mind scrambled for
the right reply. When had kids become so
complicated? "Your mom is a nice person
who cares about a lot of people, including
you." He set a root beer and a bottle opener
in front of Nick as they sat at the firehouse
kitchen table. Chad was grateful none of the

firemen were around to see him be verbally cornered by an eighth-grader. "Besides, everybody likes her."

Nick popped the cap off his root beer and folded his arms across his chest. He was silent, but the unspoken "You don't think I'm gonna fall for that, do you?" radiated from him. The dark colors he always wore looked wrong against his light skin, and seemed to clash with the bright palette of Jeannie's world. Nick had his mother's expressive eyes under all that unruly blond hair—the best features of both parents? His strong chin wasn't Jeannie's but he had her charisma already, despite the brooding wardrobe. His father must have been a good-looking man. Nick looked as though he'd grow into the kind of rugged young man high school girls swooned over. He hoped it would be the class president good guy type, but Nick's current choice of apparel hinted too much at the dark, bad boy type.

Chad sat down opposite Nick and stirred his coffee. Time for the direct approach. "We're not here to talk about your mother. We're here to talk about what made you punch Scott Collins yesterday. And why there are matches in your locker." If he was going to be direct about things, he might as well put all the issues on the table.

Nick pushed back in his chair, hands crossed over his dark gray T-shirt. "I hate when she calls me 'Nicky.'"

Chad wasn't going to let Nick detour this conversation, no matter how hard he tried. "Duly noted."

"Like I'm some kind of five-year-old." The boy had a point, but not the point in question.

"Tell her." He took a sip of coffee. "Right *after* you tell me what's going on with you in school."

"She likes you, you know." Nick leaned forward to spin the bottle cap on the table. From somewhere behind him, Chad heard Plug wander into the kitchen, and Nicky's body language immediately softened. "I heard her talking on the phone to Mrs. Reed about it, saying how she didn't know if she wanted things to get complicated, whatever that means." Nick scratched Plug's ears as the dog settled his snout onto the boy's leg. "When I asked her what she was talking about, she made up something about some church committee." He braved a look up from petting the dog. "Mom's the worst liar ever."

Chad wondered if God was toying with

him, or if Nick Nelworth was too skilled at picking distracting topics of conversation. With a sigh, he redirected the conversation back again, despite Nick's glare. "She's really worried about you. You're smart enough to know that what you did has lots of people worried." Chad leaned down to catch Nick's eye. "Look, Nick," he said, hoping the boy noticed he never called him "Nicky" and it earned points in his favor, "this isn't the time to get all silent and sneaky. What you've been through has messed up its share of grown men, men who didn't have to deal with eighth grade on top of it."

No response.

"I know from experience that if you keep that kind of stuff bottled up it's going to come out in bad ways. I think it's *already* come out in bad ways. Ways that could get worse."

Nick scuffed his shoe against the table leg and looked away. Good. He must be making a dent if Nick couldn't look at him just now. Chad shifted his weight and pressed on, startled by how badly he felt the need to make a difference in this boy's life. Only it wasn't guilt or obligation that drove it—although those things were still there—affection had grown, too. He softened his voice and leaned in. "It won't get easier. You can't ignore stuff like this. It's too big, too dark. I'm not saying you have to talk about it with your mom or even with me, but you ought to talk about it with *someone*. There's a program for kids who…"

"What?" Nick bristled. "So, you think I'm some kind of pyro, too?"

"I don't think you're a 'pyro,' Nick, but I think you need to talk to someone."

"I'm not dumb. I know what those 'programs' really are. No way am I doing anything like that."

You're thirteen. How do you know what you need? Chad thought to himself in frustration. He drew in a breath and backtracked. "Well, then, what about Pastor Allen? He's our chaplain for the firehouse, and he runs the youth programs at your church, right? He seems like an okay guy to me. Or there's Mrs. Corning."

Nick spun the cap again. "Mrs. Corning's all full of programs, too. Why can't anyone get that I don't need to talk to anyone, especially Mrs. Corning?"

Chad knew Mrs. Corning wouldn't really get him anywhere. The school counselor scented her office with potpourri, drank herbal tea and used twelve psychological buzz words per sentence. In other words, warm and fuzzy enough to grate on any thirteen-year-old boy's nerves.

"I see your point, but Scott Collins's black eye says we still have a problem." Chad leaned back in his chair, hoping to let Nick know he was ready for a long conversation. "How about we skip all the other people and programs for now and you just tell me what happened yesterday and during the fire drill earlier? I'm on your side. If you talk to me, I can help you and your mom figure out what to do from here."

There was a long, fidgety silence. Nick spun the cap over and over, but Chad discovered the boy's hesitation didn't bother him at all. It had happened again, that unexpected flash of insight. He could read Nick as easily as he read Jeannie. Nick was deciding whether or not to trust Chad. Whether or not to talk about the storm going on inside him.

Let him trust me. Chad was shocked to realize it was more of a prayer than a thought. *Please let him trust me with this.* He felt the need to say it again, sure God wasn't accustomed to paying any attention to him.

The cap turned more slowly, until it finally wobbled and fell over to chatter against the Formica tabletop. "Nobody gets it," Nick said when it stilled.

"What it's like to survive a fire, you mean?" Chad said carefully.

Nick nodded.

Thank you. That thought didn't feel odd as a prayer. *Thank you.* "I know. Everybody thinks they know how it feels, but they don't. They try to be nice, but sometimes they say stupid things, don't they?"

"Scott says stupid things all the time." Nick kept his eyes on the cap, tapping it with one finger.

Chad stayed very still. "But you don't punch him all the time. What'd he say yesterday?" Jeannie had given him the basics, but he wanted to hear Nick's own words.

"That I set the fire—the one at our house, I mean. That all this fire drill stuff was because of me. That everyone's scared I'll set the school on fire." He tapped the cap with each accusation as if jabbing a finger back at Scott Collins.

"No one thinks that." Never in the entire

investigation report—which he'd gone over twice—did anyone post any suspicions that Nick had been involved. A thirteen-year-old kid cannot manipulate faulty wiring.

No response. Chad hated that bullies like Collins knew the weak spots so well.

"You know we didn't do that assembly just because of your fire, don't you? Think back, Nick. I did that assembly at your school last year, and the year before that. It had nothing to do with you."

"It's a dumb assembly. We know that stuff already."

Chad remembered calling anything that made him uncomfortable "dumb" at that age, too. "Well, I should have changed it this year. I owe you an apology for not figuring out a way to make all of this fire safety stuff easier on you."

That got his attention. "No, you don't. You don't need to do anything. No one needs to do anything for me. There's nothing wrong with me, I'm no pyro and I don't need any stupid program, got it?" He rolled his eyes, looking like a young boy again. "Seriously."

After that speech, Chad was sure Nick would get up and walk out, but he didn't. That had to be a good sign. Moving his coffee cup aside, Chad tried a different tactic. "Did you know it took your mother four tries to light a match the other day?"

"Ha. I did it in two." Nick froze and looked up, caught.

Chad nodded. "It's not like I didn't know already. Your mom and I were testing smoke alarms, but you? You had no business doing that in school."

"*Outside* of school."

Chad glared at Nick. "Anywhere. Look, Nick, you're not some kind of freak. Fires mix up people's feelings." He thought of Jeannie's death grip on the leash as she crossed Tyler Street and how her hands shook lighting the match. "Your mom's pretty strong, and brave, but even *she's* having trouble. *I* had trouble. The only dumb thing here would be to pretend that *you're* not having trouble."

Nick forced a laugh and pointed at him. "You. You had trouble. You're a fireman."

How many times had he voiced the same thought? Firefighters felt pain the same as everyone else, only his came laced with both personal *and* professional regrets. If it took covering some uncomfortable ground to keep Nick from more pain, Chad found himself willing to speak about his past. "Some-one very close to me died in a fire. While I was just starting to be a firefighter. It made me do some really stupid things for a while." He paused for a moment before adding, "I'd like it if that didn't happen to you."

"All my stuff is gone." Nick began bouncing the cap on the table, the words finally gushing out of him. "I hate our apartment. I don't have a bus stop but driving in the Jeep is even worse. I hate how my teachers keep asking me if everything's okay. Mom's acting all weird. Every time I have a nightmare she acts like I'm gonna need to see a doctor or something. I wish everyone would *just lay off.*"

It was as if the safety valve finally opened up, letting some of the pressure off. He'd finally done something to help the kid, and it settled in his chest with a satisfied glow. "That's quite a list. I might start punching jerks if I had all that to deal with, and I know better." He caught Nick's eye with a hint of a smile. "I hope *you* know better. Your mom's just nuts and worried because she loves you. A lot. And she's hurting in her own way, you're smart enough to know that. So, the way I figure it, the smartest thing to do here would be to give her less to worry about. Right?"

Nick gave Chad the first smile he'd seen since the fight. "What'd you do? I mean, when you had your fire, what'd you do?"

I shut down my life for eight years. He was venturing into territories Chad was absolutely not ready discuss. "I didn't punch anybody, if that's what you're asking."

Nick didn't budge. He sat back again, arms across his chest. "So…what'd you do?"

"You're right. I like your mother."

Chapter Twelve

"Whoa, are these Chinese fireworks?"

Chad turned from the box of old reports he was sorting in the storage room to find Nick coming down the hall holding Helen's box of Chinese lanterns. He must have found it in the back when he was sweeping out the engine bay. "No, they're something else." He did *not* like the way Nick's face lit up at the thought of fireworks. Aside from the requisite stint riding the engine in the town parade, most firemen Chad knew weren't fond of the Fourth of July on account of the mishaps and injuries from amateur fireworks displays. Nick Nelworth would not add himself to that list if Chad had anything to do with it.

Nick set the box down and squatted beside it. "So, what are they?"

"They're some things a friend sent."

"You have friends in China?" To Chad's dismay, Nick was peering into the part of the box top Chad had opened to pull out what he had come to call "Helen's Annual Letter." He'd been smart enough to extract that little emotional time bomb before bringing the box to the firehouse, but it now left an entryway big enough for Nick's hand to pry the box open farther. "What's in here?"

Chad realized that his earlier answer had been a mistake; there wasn't any way to explain what the intriguing box was—and why his name was on the delivery label—without talking about Laurie. He wondered if this was God's way of telling him "opening up and talking about it" was a two-way street. With a resigned sigh, Chad pushed his file box back onto the dusty shelf and walked toward Nick. "Okay, come here and I'll show you."

Chad led Nick out onto the bench in front of the firehouse, out in the sunshine because it felt better to talk about it outside. Not just because it put them away from prying ears, but also because being under the big bright sky always made him feel smaller and less burdened.

"In China," he began, completely unsure

how he was going to go about this, "there's a holiday sometime in February."

"But it's September."

This was going to be harder than Chad thought. "I'm getting to that. Anyway, the holiday is a way to remember people who've died. Sort of like we do on Memorial Day, but it's everyone, not just soldiers. They pray and send good wishes by lighting paper lanterns that float up into the sky. In fact, part of the legend is that when people were hiding from some bad guys in the mountains, villagers sent these types of lanterns up to let them know it was safe to come home." Chad wasn't sure that was entirely accurate, but it was close enough for the eighth grade.

Nick started pulling the box open. The sound of the tape ripping mirrored the sensation in Chad's chest. "I don't get it. Why is someone from China sending you lanterns for dead people?"

No, this wasn't going to be easy at all. "The lanterns aren't really for the dead people. They're for the people still alive, as a way of remembering." That sounded exactly like something Helen would have said; she'd be smiling if she knew this conversation was taking place. Maybe even laughing. Still, his chest felt tight.

Nick managed to pull out one of the paper lanterns—why Helen sent multiples, he never knew—and pulled the circular rings until the paper globe took shape. "Neat. I like these. They're like little hot air balloons."

"Scientifically speaking, that's exactly what they are. You send them up at night, so they're kind of like flares, too, because they glow. Well, that's what I've seen in the pictures—I've never actually sent one up."

Nick thought that was absurd. "Why not? They're cool. So you don't have anyone dead to remember?"

Talk about a loaded question. Chad couldn't help but wonder if God had sent a thirteen-year-old to corner him on purpose, or if it just worked out that way. "I do." It felt hard to even say that much. It meant a further explanation would now be unavoidable.

Nick looked at him, awareness dawning in his eyes so that he looked all too much like his mother. "In the fire? The one you talked about?"

Chad pushed the words up from the torn place in his chest. "Her name was Laurie, and we were going to be married, but she died before the wedding." Chad took the paper globe from Nick just to have something other than the boy's wide blue eyes to look at. "Laurie's mom is Chinese, and she sends me these every year."

"So you can remember her."

As if I would ever forget her. "Yes."

There was a long silence. Chad waited for the ripping to get worse, for the huge slam of the pain to hit him, to take over and swallow him up, but it didn't. There was a deep ache, a surge of regret, but it wasn't shattering. Nick took another lantern out of the box and pulled it open. He found the candlelike fixture that went on the bottom and figured out how it attached without even reading the instructions. "I like these. Do you think I could have one to remember my dad?"

Chad didn't even have to think about it. "Absolutely." It would be like Jeannie's birthday candle, redeeming flame for him in a positive way instead of a weapon against the anger.

"Mom would love these."

Chad had the exact same thought. Suddenly, the ritual made sense, and launching the lanterns with Jeannie and Nick seemed the most natural thing in the world. As if the box had been waiting for them. "You're right," he said, finding the lump in his throat entirely too sentimental. When Nick pretended to make the globe float up into the air, Chad had a vision of Jeannie in the evening, illuminated by the glow of the lanterns as they floated up into the night, and the lump in his throat got larger.

"And we all got people to remember, so it kinda works out." Nick leaned his shoulder into Chad.

It was so simple. Nick said it as if their collective losses were a binding force, not a weight to be borne alone—again, something Helen would have said. He remembered the photos of the ceremony with hundreds of lanterns floating up into the sky and out over the water, and it no longer seemed like a silly stunt, but rather a touching tribute. Certainly more fitting than any of the dry memorial services he'd endured for Laurie and absolutely the kind of thing Jeannie would adore. "I suppose it does." He hoped his voice didn't betray the emotions whirling around inside. It was so much easier when all that stayed stuffed down. And yet, hadn't he just told Nick how damaging it was to keep things stuffed down?

Nick fitted the candle piece into the globe and held it up with satisfaction. It looked exactly like a miniature hot air balloon. "So when do we launch them—you, me and Mom?"

Chad hadn't heard a more appealing—or more dangerous—idea in years. "I'll let you know."

He hadn't planned it. It just happened, as if his feet involuntarily slipped into the back of Gordon Falls Community Church that evening.

He and Laurie had attended a big, splashy church—she loved the vitality, but he found the energy overwhelming in his grief. A handful of the firemen attended this weekly prayer service, so he'd known about it for months. This church was simple, classic in its outlay, subtle in its decor except for the vibrant stained-glass windows which even now were somber at dusk. A young woman with a pretty voice was leading praise songs at a piano in the front corner. Nothing too upbeat, just quiet and comforting.

He'd thought once or twice about coming, but never made it farther than fleeting consideration. He wasn't completely sure why he was here now. After his experience with Nick this afternoon, faith felt both a thousand miles away and almost within reach.

Chad nodded silently to the handful of familiar faces on the far left side of the room, but mostly he felt on display. A foreigner or, worse yet, an impostor. Was tonight a mistake? Or the first right step in a long time?

The woman up front announced the next song, and he was relieved it was one he recognized. He didn't sing, and he was sure it would hurt to listen because he could almost hear Laurie's voice next to him. To his surprise, the words and music just flowed gently over him. No threat, no condemnation for the years he'd missed—it was as if the room somehow quietly made space for him. By the following song, the tension left his shoulders and he stopped worrying about what anyone around him was doing. He allowed himself the long-forgotten thought that God might be here, listening to the songs of these friends and neighbors, granting the peace and strength he used to draw from places like this.

It wasn't his and Laurie's church, but it couldn't have been—shouldn't have been like his and Laurie's church. He could almost feel that it was all right to be here without Laurie, that it might actually be good to be here without her. Maybe here he could begin to do this on his own. Maybe he could begin to find whatever faith he would someday call his.

Pastor Allen announced the first reading, Psalm 66, and Chad fingered the Bible tucked in its little shelf in the pew in front of him. Did he even know where his was? Helen had taken Laurie's, but he was sure he owned one once. Chad watched his hands take hold of the Bible and open it up as if they were attached to some other man. A long-ago version of himself remembered the Psalms were in the middle. It was a place to start, a foothold of his very own.

He had almost slipped out unnoticed at the service's end when Pastor Allen caught him at the door. Allen was close to Paul's age, had served as the firehouse chaplain, but Chad had steered clear of him since his arrival in Gordon Falls.

"It's good to see you here, Chad." Allen's greeting was warm enough. No "Nice of you to finally show up" like he'd expected.

"Yeah, well, I thought I'd come check things out."

Allen smiled. "Everything to your liking?"

Chad looked around, not really wanting to meet the man's eyes. "I don't know exactly what I'm looking for, so I suppose it's good so far." That sounded foolish, but Chad was stumped how to begin any kind of conversation like this.

Allen just continued smiling and nodded toward the hallway at the back of the church. "Why don't you come in for a bit?"

Some part of him knew if he followed Allen now, the whole story would come spilling out of him, as if it would take the town's big green floodgates to hold it all back.

He was weary of holding it all back. "Okay," Chad heard himself say, even though half of him yelped "No!"

The minister stopped at a kitchenette halfway down the hall and filled a coffee mug, pointing to another mug with a raised eyebrow until Chad declined the unspoken offer. "Funny you should show up today. Abby Reed was just telling me you've been quite a help to the Nelworth boy."

"Oh, I don't know that I've helped at all." Chad wasn't pleased that word had gotten out about Nick's "giant detention."

"Spending time with a fatherless boy in

a tight spot is a great big help." The word "fatherless" was like a poke in the ribs, and Chad wondered if Jeannie felt the same twinge anytime anyone mentioned Nick's late father. Allen pushed open his office door. "I can think of ten other boys who would be in much better places in this world if someone would just pay enough attention." He sighed as he sat down on a long maroon couch opposite the armchair Chad had chosen. "But somehow I don't think you came to pray for teen counseling advice." He held Chad's gaze with steady, welcoming eyes. "You look like a man with a lot on his mind."

How do you start a conversation like this? Explain a gap in your life you can't explain? Chad ran his hands down his face and reached for the words. "It's been a long time since I went to church. I mean a really long time."

Allen settled in. "I'm not much on measuring time away. I find it doesn't really matter. I'm more interested in why you left and what's drawing you back."

Chad told the shortest version of Laurie's loss and his eight-year church exile he could manage. It wasn't like opening up the floodgates; the words came with sadness, with weight, but with something closer to ease. They didn't choke him like they used to, and the slam of pain that hadn't come when he told Nick didn't come now.

"That's a lot of pain for one man to shoulder," Allen said quietly. "When's the last time you talked to anyone about losing Laurie in that fire?"

Chad actually felt a smile crack through the fog of sadness. "I told a thirteen-year-old boy about it just this afternoon."

Allen put down his coffee cup. "I think you're even a bigger help to Nick Nelworth than Abby makes you out to be. Are you ready to believe that God brought the two of you together?"

Chad shrugged. "Seems a bit epic for someone with my resume. I'm not really the guy to..." To what? He didn't have an ending for that sentence.

"Oh, from where I sit, it seems like you're just the guy."

"What makes you say that?"

"For starters, you're here." He ran his finger around the handle of the coffee mug he'd just set down. "You said you felt like your faith left you when Laurie died. Where do you think your faith went?"

"Gone. Just poof and gone. Like it couldn't hold up to what was going on." That didn't sit right as the words came out. "No, that wasn't really it." Chad relaxed into the chair, taking his grip off the armrests before confessing, "I don't really think I had any in the first place. It mostly seeped off of Laurie into me. Borrowed."

"Not really. More like shared. Being close to people of faith wakes us up to our own needs, I think. We start to want what we see in them. My own faith started as more of an admiration of my father's than any big revelation of my own."

"Yes, that's sort of it. I want what Laurie had, but well, I don't know if I can get there without her. Like I can't possibly do it on my own."

Allen leaned toward Chad. "Actually, I think the only way any of us can get there is on our own. Your faith has to be yours. It won't look or act or feel like Laurie's because it's a relationship between God and you."

"I don't know that I'm ready."

"Who ever is?" Allen managed a chuckle. "God never seems to care about 'ready,' only about 'willing.' The hardest part is getting though the door the first time, so you're half-way home."

"Are you sure this is a good idea?" Jeannie questioned Abby as she looked up from the pan of caramelizing sugar. Abby had dropped by the church kitchen as Jeannie was cooking to replenish gift basket stocks. "Yes, Saturday dinner is definitely on. Even expelled boys have to eat," Abby reasoned. She pulled on a pair of plastic food service gloves and began helping Jeannie crush pecans. Abby was the best kind of friend. Even when things were at their worst, Abby had a way of making Jeannie feel like everything was under control and things would turn out fine. During the hardest days after Henry died, Abby invited Jeannie over for coffee as always. As if everything were still normal and Jeannie's world hadn't just exploded into a million painful pieces. "You said yourself," Abby went on as she whacked at a bag with a wooden mallet, "Nick's stint at the fire station yesterday went well. Think of this as a thank-you dinner."

"That's a bit of a stretch." Still, her son seemed less dark, less tense. Jeannie checked the candy thermometer clipped to the side of the saucepan. "Nicky is actually excited at the idea of having dinner with Chad." Nicky had actually smiled today, hinting at some kind of plan the two of them were hatching, although she had no idea what.

"The man is helping your son." Abby poured out the bag of pieces into a stainless-steel bowl and refilled the bag with whole nuts. "The least we can do is feed him." Abby was clearly not giving in.

Chad *was* helping her son, and that meant the world to her. But Jeannie was aware that her feelings for Chad were gathering a little too much momentum.

Abby pounded for a few seconds, then stopped to point the mallet handle at Jeannie. "It's not going to go away, you know."

Jeannie returned her gaze to the thermometer, willing the correct temperature, the one requiring immediate action, to appear *now*. "What isn't?"

"What's going on between you two. What's going on between you three, actually. Did it ever occurred to you that Frank and I have been praying for something like this for years? He went to church last night, did you know that?"

Jeannie leaned against the counter, suddenly exhausted from all the inner turmoil. Chad went to church. She was glad—truly, deeply glad—but in truth, it only made things more complicated. "That doesn't make everything clear between us. And the timing is still, well, horrible. I don't know what to do." She checked the other pan of ingredients, stirring it once. Timing how one blended ingredients was crucial to candies. And life. Half of her wanted to rush forward and give in to whatever this thing was blooming between her and Chad Owens. The other half of her wanted to run away from the new storm of feelings surging up inside her. "Why does it feel like God had pulled every rug out from underneath me all at once?"

"I don't know, Jeannie. You've been through enough heartbreak for four lifetimes. I told God He needs to let up, if that makes any difference."

The necessary temperature achieved, Jeannie carefully poured the creamy mixture into the bubbling sugar, reveling in the aroma. She was good at this, very good. She stirred until just the right color appeared in the pot, then turned down the heat for the several minutes of the final step. "I can't help thinking Nicky's through the worst of it. It's simply got to get better from here." Her eye caught a batch of photographs held to the church fridge with a magnet, the satisfying scent warring with a sudden sharp loss for all the kindergarten and first grade photos lost to ashes forever. The baby pictures. The wedding pictures. "He's...well, it's a vulnerable time for him. For me. I can't add a complicated relationship. I can't risk losing my focus on Nicky by getting myself in a tangle. I need to see the clear path right now."

"And what if the clear path is through Chad Owens?"

That was the least calming thought of all. Jeannie was taking a breath to say maybe it would be better to just wait a week when Abby started whacking again. "Don't you even think of canceling. And wear something nice. And bring some of these. They smell wonderful."

Nicky gave her an incredulous glance when she came out of her bedroom Saturday night dressed in a new yellow sweater. Fine time for Nicky to decide to start noticing what she wore.

"What?" she challenged as they pulled their coats on. "I was saving this for a week when I needed cheering up."

"Yeah," he replied, drawing out the word in awful teen cynicism, hinting at a million things in one syllable.

Dinner felt remarkably easy. Frank and Chad evidently had several things in common, and Abby's high school senior son, Ben, scooped up Nicky as always. Ben referred to Nicky as his "honorary little brother," and the boys got along famously.

"It would help if Ben were a little *less* impressed with Nicky's expulsion," Jeannie joked to Abby as they set out slices of cake and a bowl of Jeannie's chocolate covered sea-salt caramels after dinner.

"Well, I agree, but think of it this way. Ben's just first in line to assure you Nicky's future hasn't tanked. Ben still thinks he's cool, it's just that now he's gained an additional sort of 'cool' *most* of us would rather he'd have avoided. Here," she said, popping one of the caramels into her mouth with an appreciative moan, "take these to the Nick Nelworth Admiration Society downstairs."

Jeannie felt Chad come up behind her as she stood at the top of the den stairs. She'd

been watching Nick and Ben as they de-
voured cake between bursts of video-game
combat. Chad looked down at the boys as
well, tucking his hands into the pocket of
the olive-colored corduroy pants he wore.
He wore a tan shirt, the henley kind with
no collar and a handful of buttons at the
neck, and the way he pushed the sleeves
up made his arms look lean and strong. He
was chewing, and she could tell he had one
of her caramels in his mouth. It was an unnerving thought. He had a way of looking
grounded and sad, as if nothing could ever
unsettle him. She knew, though, by the way
he'd spoken so painfully of his past, that his
sullen stability came at a very high cost.

"Peas in a pod, those two," Jeannie said
as Ben cuffed Nicky playfully, the two of
them erupting in laughter and taunts over
the game.

"Yep," he said as he polished off the last of
the caramel. Jeannie loved to watch people
tasting her candy. She jokingly called it "the
caramel swoon" when people rolled their
eyes shut in pleasure after popping one of
her famous caramels into their mouths. She
wasn't at all ready to think of Chad Owens
doing "the caramel swoon."

He didn't look like he swooned over anything. She saw hints of pleasure in his face, but a bitter resignation always clung to the edge of his eyes. The boys burst out laughing again, bringing a wide smile from her but only the start of one from Chad. Nicky had said he'd laughed yesterday. She found herself envious that her son had heard Chad's laughter but she had not.

"He talked to me yesterday," he offered, eyes on the boys. "Told me about what's been going on at school, how he's been feeling, what's bugging him. Not much, but the wall came down for a minute or two." Chad looked up at her, and she saw how much Nicky had come to mean to Chad.

Chad Owens, the last person she'd ever have thought, cared about her son. A great deal from the looks of it. Something broke loose in her heart, the last of her resistance slipped down without her permission. At that moment, Ben scored some victory, which sent the boys tumbling over each other in shouts and good-natured tussling. For the first time since Mrs. Hunnington's awful phone call, Jeannie felt weight slide from her shoulders. Maybe Nicky would really be okay after all. Maybe she didn't need all the answers just yet.

"He's a great kid, your son." There was a lot behind those words. Far better than any caramel swoon.

"He thinks you're great." She could see the veil of pain come down over his eyes at the mention of Nicky's admiration, and thought maybe Abby was right; maybe and all this with Nicky was "the clear path," and not just for her. What if they were also part of Chad's journey back into his faith? She found that enormously satisfying. "He looks up to you. You know that."

A storm of emotion tumbled through his mossy eyes. He was uncomfortable with how much Nicky looked up to him, but at the same time too pleased to deny it. How had she ever thought this man so one-dimensional? How had she never seen past the gruff facade before when it seemed too obvious now?

"Knock it off down there, you boys!" came Frank's voice from the kitchen behind them. "You've got the full moon in the both of you and Ben has already broken the coffee table once this year."

"Full moon?" Chad peered up through the

back door window on the landing behind him. "Oh, she's a beauty. Harvest moon, I think." He turned and looked at her, his eyes doing wild things to her pulse. He licked a smear of chocolate from his finger and Jeannie felt her own "caramel swoon."

She knew what he was going to say before he said it. "Want to go see?" he almost whispered.

"Sure," Jeannie heard herself whisper back, not objecting when Chad grabbed a plaid wool blanket from a set of hooks on the nearby wall. She nearly giggled when he opened the door and she swept out into the night.

Chapter Thirteen

The whole night Chad had known he was slipping, falling for her in a way that would irrevocably tangle his life with Jeannie's and Nick's. When she'd ducked outside to do something so hopelessly romantic as to see the moon, he didn't stand a chance. He hadn't from the beginning.

With that confounded resolution of hers, she'd leaped across the chasm he couldn't. She slowed her steps away from the house until he'd caught up to her, and then promptly slipped her hand into his. The whole world skidded to a halt around them. Jeannie held his hand, Jeannie had *taken* his hand by her own choice. The other night he'd touched her, but tonight *she'd touched him*.

He pulled her a few paces away from the

light of the house, then turned to wrap the red plaid blanket more tightly around her shoulders. The need to keep her safe and warm warred with the urge to keep her here under the night sky. They might only have a few minutes, but the dark stillness seemed to be arranged perfectly around them, the moonlight like something out of a Van Gogh painting. Countless stars hovered overhead, the vastness of the universe spread possibilities in every direction. He wanted to see her in this moonlight more than he wanted to be strong or sensible. She was so delicately beautiful, he was sure he'd break her heart.

He pulled in a breath to tell her to stay away, but couldn't form the words. Jeannie Nelworth was turning him inside out.

He'd barely been able to contain the urge to wrap her in his arms when they were in her kitchen the other night. He'd thought about the feel of her hair falling over her shoulders, the way it brushed against his hand as he touched her, nearly every waking moment since it happened. His growing affection for Nick made the red sirens going off in his head hard to bear. Did his professional involvement—though he was involved now, totally, completely, personally involved—mean he should keep an objective distance?

He still wasn't sure why she'd asked him to leave that night. Was it because she didn't want to hear his suspicions? Or was it because now was not the time for them to get into a complicated relationship? Neither changed the fact he knew—absolutely—that she felt something for him. She just said yes now with eyes that told him she wanted to be near him.

"You were in church last night." It seemed unrelated, but then again, not for Jeannie. Had that been what changed her mind? Her faith was everything to her; she'd need someone who could share that.

"Yes."

"What made you come back?"

How had she known it was a return for him? "At first I told myself it was just to show Nick that church was where he should turn when things got tough."

Her eyes grew wide and lush. "You went for Nicky? You'd do that for him?"

"It was way more than that. I couldn't come back before, but lately, it's been as if I couldn't *help* but come back. You and Nick had a lot…so much…to do with that." Would she realize what an enormous admission that was? He saw so much of God's spirit in her. Now, tonight, now he realized how badly he wanted *her* to lead him back toward his own lost faith. *Rescue me,* he wanted to whisper into her hair.

He wasn't supposed to get a second chance at this. She needed someone with less damage, someone who could match her joy at life. "Tell me to go away, and I will. You and Nick need...well, you don't need someone like me."

"Nicky needs you. And I..." She didn't finish, just looked at him. He was tumbling off the edge of the highest cliff and he knew it. He relished it.

The blanket slipped off her shoulders and he quickly ducked to bring it back around her. The gesture placed his arms around her, and he was lost for certain. "Jeannie," he gulped out, the curve of her shoulders under his hands driving him mad. She brought her hand up to rest against his cheek, and Chad actually felt his head spin. He'd thought this kind of thing was gone for him forever, but it wasn't. She was here, now, nearly glowing in the moonlight and laying her impossibly smooth hand against his cheek. He found himself as desperate to kiss her as a high-schooler, but would not allow himself to give in until he knew she felt the same. *Please let her feel the same.*

The flush in her cheeks had nothing to do with the cold, their breath tumbled frosty-white in the air as he pulled her just the tiniest bit closer. "Chad," she whispered as he lost himself in those huge brown eyes, "you better kiss me now or I think I'll just about die."

"Don't die." He realized he was smiling. Grinning like a fool, actually. She felt the same.

"Don't wait." She wrapped her arms around his neck and he had just enough composure to catch the blanket as it nearly fell again before he leaned in and let his lips brush across hers. She shivered slightly in his arms, and that was the end of all reason. Chad pulled the blanket around the two of them, taking her into his arms and giving in to the blinding bliss of kissing her. She was soft and warm. She felt exquisite in his arms, perfect and delicate and stirring up such heat he felt he could stay out here a week.

Still, it was about so much more than heat. She was sweet, courageous and so full of light that her touch seemed to crack open parts of him that had been dark for ages. When he kissed her, he touched the spark of life that always seemed to surround her, and he felt that energy spark him to life.

She was beautiful, but it wasn't her appearance that intrigued him. It was her strength and vibrancy, the most lovable tenacity he'd ever known in a woman. In anyone. He could love her, someday, if he healed enough. Right now, with the moonlight shimmering in her hair, he prayed that he would heal enough to love this woman and her son.

Jeannie melted against his chest, snuggling into the blanket as he wrapped her closer. "I think I just forgot how to breathe," she said softly. Was that his heart slamming against his chest or hers?

He took a deep breath of his own. "They'll... um...miss us," he said, somehow coming to his senses before the scent of her hair stole his last scrap of reason. "We should go inside."

"We should." There was that butterscotch smile of hers again. He couldn't help smiling himself. Smiling. When was the last time he'd done that? Out of nowhere, an idea tempted him: forget every obligation, every worry, every task and simply walk with her through the moonlit pines that filled Frank's backyard. *A woman who paints her Jeep in polka dots can do that to you,* he chided himself, unsettled at how much appeal the crazy idea held. Chad Owens was the kind of man who filed reports, not the kind of man who stole kisses in the dark.

He stole three more before they went inside.

Monday was Nicky's least favorite school day—math test day—but it also meant his return to class. Piled on top of everything else, it made for a complicated morning. Jeannie's spirit waffled between concern for Nicky and a giddy wonder over Saturday night. She watched Nicky's every movement for some confirmation that things would be okay from here, but couldn't read him. His spirit had seemed lighter over the weekend, but the threat of Monday's return to school had rendered him dark and grumpy again last night. "Teenagers are like a roller coaster," Abby had consoled. If the ups and downs were this bad in eighth grade, Jeannie wasn't sure how she was going to make it through his high school years.

"Can I have some coffee?" Nicky wandered in looking rumpled and surly in black jeans and a dark brown shirt with some video game logo on the back. It startled her how much older he looked in dark colors.

"Coffee? Absolutely not. You've thirteen, for goodness' sake."

"I'll be in high school soon."

Oh, how she was aware of that fact. Jeannie stared into her coffee as Nicky got out the cereal—a sugary, kid cereal she noticed with a satisfied smirk.

She'd been thinking about Chad all morning, and Nicky had noticed. More than once her son had looked up from his cereal to give her the same exasperated look he usually reserved for pink objects, anything with ruffles or his grandmother's cheek pinches.

"I thought you told me Chad was coming to our church now."

"I did. He went Thursday night, Mrs. Reed said."

"So where was he yesterday?" he asked behind an enormous mouthful of cereal.

So he had looked for Chad, too? "Well, Chief Bradens was missing as well, so maybe there was something going on over at the firehouse." Chad couldn't have been avoiding her, could he? Oh, goodness, now who was acting like a teenager? Nicky seemed to somehow know her tension had a new and unfamiliar layer. "He's nice," she offered, groping some parentally wise way to raise such a difficult subject.

Nicky just grunted.

Jeannie had no idea how to handle the prospect of a new man in her life. She still had to deal with his school issues, emotional tangles or no. They ended up driving to school in near silence.

"Nicky," she began as she pulled up in the school drive, "make sure Mrs. Hunnington—"

"Got it, Mom," he cut in sharply.

She went to hand him his backpack, but he snatched it from the backseat before she could reach it. "You still have to serve deten—"

"I *know,* Mom," Nicky barked at her as he lifted the door latch, obviously not wanting her to raise the subject.

Well, he wasn't going to get his way. This was too important a juncture for him, too much at stake. He was sliding out of the car when she caught his elbow. Nicky groaned and swiveled his head back to glare at her.

Jeannie refused to back down. "Now look here, Nicky…"

He threw his hand in the air. "Stop calling me Nicky! Just stop calling me that!"

It was like getting the wind knocked out of her. They both sat stunned for a second. Jeannie swallowed, grappling to keep her composure. "Nicholas Nelworth," she said as evenly as she could manage, "you made a big mistake. You know that, and what's done is done. But you've also been given a second chance. I expect you to make the most of it."

Nicky merely grunted and pulled out of the car. *Watch over him, Lord,* she prayed as she watched him shuffle up the sidewalk, all dark-jeaned and bushy-haired. It was as if someone threw a mysterious internal switch on her son, kicking him over into the teenage years before either of them was ready. *Oh, Lord, watch over all of us. It's gotten so complicated all of a sudden.*

She said a dozen other prayers as she made the short drive from school to the Sweet Treats renovation site. Things in her life had grown wonderfully and immensely complicated at the same time. Her heart leaped as she pulled the Jeep into the parking space in front of Sweet Treats—not only because of her beautiful new front door, but because Abby was there with a steaming cup of coffee in each hand.

"You have the most wonderful gift of showing up when you're needed," Jeannie said with a tired sigh as she unlocked the new door.

"That bad, huh?" Abby followed inside.

"What happened to my nice little boy? It's like sharing an apartment with a porcupine." She looked at the new display racks leaning up against the wood studs and wished for a time machine to whoosh her directly to the store's opening. It killed her not to be able to work in here, live in here. She could only visit, and that was like being asked to visit paradise but never stay. To stand in here and feel her future so clearly made the tiny beige apartment all the more painful.

"In a word? Hormones." Abby shucked her jacket and wandered over to look at the racks. "Well, that and a lot of other stuff. You're in the parenting Olympics here, girl. You can't get discouraged if things don't go perfectly. You've gone from cute and cuddly to dark and prickly, and it doesn't let up for another eight years or so...if then."

Jeannie drowned her apprehensions a gulp

of the delicious coffee. Once Sweet Treats opened, it would be a particular blessing that Karl's Koffee was exactly halfway between here and Abby's craft store. "Oh, cuddly is definitely off the table. And as for perfection? I think we're looking at pure survival."

"Has he stopped hugging you yet?"

Jeannie swallowed hard. "They stop?"

Abby sighed. "For a while. Punches you in the gut, it does. I used to think the moms who went in to hug their teenagers while they were sleeping were nuts."

Jeannie did not like the look in Abby's eyes. "Have you?"

"Only twice. Now I just demand he hugs me and pretend that I can't see his tortured expression."

"I'm so glad you're funny, even when you're sad." She hugged Abby enough for three sons. "You're the perfect laugh I needed this morning."

Abby turned her gaze out the window to the fire station. "Speaking of perfection, you were looking perfectly smitten Saturday night. I take it things are going well between you and Chad?"

She spoke as if they were already a certified couple. Were they? It was so hard to tell. "He is so different than what I thought, Abby."

Abby shot her a look as she sipped her coffee. "You're positively grinning. I'll take that to mean he's so much *better* than you thought?"

Leaning back against one of the columns, Jeannie wondered if she could even put her confusion into words. "I don't know. There's so much in our pasts. He lost someone very close to him in a fire, did you know that?"

Abby shook her head. "I figured it was something like that, but it makes sense. You two have a great deal in common. And as for tough pasts, well, that's what futures are for."

"It feels too early to be thinking about that kind of future. He's still so distant in some ways, as if he's always fighting something dark coming up from behind him."

Abby smiled at Jeannie. "I can't think of anybody better to lighten up a life than you. I'd say it's time you both got your second helpings of happiness in this world."

"I suppose."

"You're not some love-struck teenagers. You know the real thing when you see it and you know where to be careful. You both go deeper than that. So don't be afraid of being happy instead of just being cheerful, Jeannie. God's not done with either of you yet by a long shot." She took another gulp of coffee and looked around. "Speaking of not being done, how *is* the store coming?"

"Ugh." Jeannie set her coffee down on a sawhorse. "Hurdle after hurdle."

Abby picked up a swatch of fabric sitting on the windowsill. "This is adorable."

"It would be, if it weren't on back-order. Two pieces of equipment, too. And then there's the insurance company, which wants still more paperwork." She closed her eyes, picturing how the sun would come in through the kitchen windows upstairs where she planned to use the same fabric. How clearly she could imagine herself coming down the back stairway with enormous steaming mug of coffee in her hand as she opened up the shop each morning. "It kills me not to be in here, Abby. This place feels so much more like home than where we are now. That stupid occupancy permit. I can barely work in here, I can't live in here and all because I've got no occupancy permit. Not yet. Oh, how I grown to hate the words 'not yet.'"

"It'll get here. You know it will. It just will take time. Have you taken time to talk to Chad this morning?"

Jeannie managed a weak laugh. "Not yet. What a surprise that man is."

"Yes, so you said. Twice."

"I'm that obvious?"

Abby smiled. "It's nice to see. Really. Okay, maybe a bit on the smitten side, but I'll look past it for now."

Jeannie's gaze wandered across the street to the firehouse. "Oh, Abby, I don't know if there's really something there."

"Believe me, it looks like there's definitely something there. Was it a good kiss?"

Jeannie glared at her friend.

"Hey, it's a big kitchen window and it was a big, bright moon. A big, bright *romantic* moon. It wasn't like I was watching once I heard the back door open."

Jeannie glared again.

"Much."

Talking about kisses felt like something out of high school. "Something happened in him. I mean, yes, it's obvious he has feelings for me, but he resisted at first."

"So *you* kissed *him?*" Abby rocked back on one hip. "Good for you."

"Then, it was as if something gave way in him. It was intense. Desperate, even, and I was sure my knees were going to go out from underneath me. It was wonderful." Jeannie closed her eyes, remembering how her head spun back there in the moonlight. "But a second later—" she felt herself flush "—okay, maybe a lot more than a second, it was as if some alarm went off inside him. I could feel him retreat, Abby. Go all tense and sad. I think he wasn't restraining himself, he was *denying* himself. As if he wasn't allowed to kiss me or be close to me."

"So he's complicated. Complications don't usually scare you—you threw yourself into remodeling this place without a moment's hesitation."

"I'm analyzing this too much, aren't I?"

Abby sat down on the windowsill. "Look, Jeannie, you're allowed to kiss a man and you know what's at stake here. What you're *not* allowed to do is let what might be a very good thing pass you by just because it's complicated. The only way you'll ever know for sure if this is a good thing is to spend less time with this lumber—" she pointed around the room "—and spend more time with that man." She pointed to the firehouse.

"I know, I know, but I have to go out to Richmond Farms this morning."

"So, ask him to go with you." Abby stood up. "He's friends with Mike Richmond, isn't he? Go spend some time, just the two of you."

Jeannie sank onto a sawhorse, clutching her coffee cup. "It's really the only way to figure this out, isn't it? I knew that. Somewhere in here I knew that."

Abby headed toward the door. "So get out of here and go do something about it." When Jeannie hesitated, she reached out and pulled her friend off the sawhorse. "As in *now*."

Chapter Fourteen

"Good morning," Chad said, pulling open the door even before she got to it. It was his voice, and then again an entirely different voice. A warmer, sunnier version of the voice she'd heard Saturday night. He wore a royal blue sweater, and she wondered if it was just her imagination, or if she'd ever seen him in a bright color before. His eyes were clearer, and it was as if his whole face had changed—but then again, it hadn't. There was so much about him that now seemed completely different. "Everything okay?"

Did he mean her? Nicky? The store? She nodded, flustered. He flashed a sheepish, confused grin, as if to say, "I don't know how to do this, either," then ushered her into the office. "Nick make it to school all right?" Had he always smelled so wonderful? Or did he just stand closer to her now?

She shrugged her shoulders. "He's grumpy, but at least he's there." Chad's hand feathered across her shoulder as he took her coat, and Jeannie felt her heart do a little flip. "He suspects something," she went on, sure her grin must look childish. "He looked at me this morning with one of those looks. The ones reserved for gushy stuff he can't stand."

He grimaced, but it was more playful than pained. Embarrassed, actually, which was exactly how she felt. Giddy felt ridiculous for her age, but it was clear he was as unfamiliar with all this as she. "Gushy stuff like…"

"Us," she finished for him, then regretted it. Were they an "us" already? To Abby, maybe, but she wasn't so sure. There was no way to deny how significant Saturday night had been—for either of them. Some moments, it felt like the whole world shifted under that moon. Other times, it didn't feel sudden at all, but built up over fateful, chosen moments. However it came to be, it was not something casual. It was huge and powerful. Was that good or bad? "It's a lot to take in," she backpedaled, thinking that sounded like the most inane thing ever to leave her mouth.

"It is." His face was impossible to read.

You've been given a second chance, I expect you to make the most of it. She'd settled for a life alone with Nicky, living on gratitude and memory. Maybe it really was time to rebuild more than just the store. "Are you free this morning? I've got to run out to Richmond Farms and I..." She felt so very awkward all of a sudden. "I thought you could come with me."

He looked startled, as if it was the last thing he expected to hear from her. Which made sense, because she could barely believe she was doing it herself.

"Really?"

He wanted to come—that much was obvious—but something was holding him back. It was like watching Saturday night play out all over again across his face. "Yeah, really," she blurted out. "If you know you're free and all."

He took an excruciatingly long time to answer. "I've got paperwork." Jeannie felt her heart collapse like a house of cards. "But it can wait."

* * *

Chad couldn't believe he was actually nervous. He was glad he insisted he do the driving out to Mike Richmond's farm. Not only because he was certain he wasn't yet up to riding in the polka-dotted Jeep, but driving simply gave him something to do. Goofy paint job aside, he was sure he'd have gone crazy just sitting in the passenger seat. There was no need for directions; besides George, Mike was the closest thing he had to a friend in Gordon Falls. All of which made showing up at Richmond Farms with a pretty lady rather nerve-wracking. Especially when that pretty lady had done the inviting.

Mike's apple orchard also hosted the region's most popular farmers' market in the summer season. The picturesque old farm looked like something out of a movie set as he pulled his truck into the gravel drive. The trees still boasted fall's last bursts of color, trimmed as they were with frost. The air smelled crisp and potent—fall's intoxicating aroma that drew tourists from all over Illinois and the surrounding states. Mike had some animals—mostly for atmosphere rather than any serious livestock—apples and honey were his focus. Jeannie told him she was coming out to begin restoring her stock of Mike's excellent honey, but during the drive Chad had hatched a plan his own involving another bee byproduct.

It was fun to watch Jeannie in her element. She darted in and out of the farm's storehouse and small retail shop like, well, like a kid in a candy store. "I'm going to need two cases of that." "Who's your supplier for these?" "I've got to carry this in the store when it opens!" And he let her energy seep into him. The woman tinted the whole world yellow when she was fired up like that. With a jolt of fear, Chad realized he was coming to crave her vibrance. He'd woken up in the middle of the night finding it too dark, missing how she lit up his world. Already, she felt too precious, too important. Strong as he knew she was, she seemed too fragile for the likes of him; he'd go mad if anything happened to her.

His breath caught when she grabbed his hand as Mike lifted the lid off a crate of raw honeycomb for her to see. Chad tensed, not ready to let even an old friend like Mike see him holding Jeannie's hand, sure he'd never be able to hide his affections. It felt like Gordon Falls's own floodgates could no longer keep back what was surging between them. He needn't have worried; Mike threw him a wink and an approving nod over Jeannie's head as she bent down to inspect the comb further. The fact that it made things with Nicky more complicated no longer mattered; he simply couldn't help himself.

He could, however, help her. He'd devised a plan to finish what the birthday candles had started. Chad nodded at Mike who, with a conspiratorial grin, pushed open a door to the workroom behind him. "One of the very best things you can do with beeswax," Mike began, acting on the request Chad made half an hour ago while Jeannie wasn't looking, "is to make candles."

"You told me you used to love candles... before. I thought making a set of beeswax candles might help things along." Chad knew it would work, as if God himself pushed the idea into his head. Once Chad finally got up the nerve to cross the threshold into church last week, it was as if God eagerly resumed their relationship. As if all the years of Chad ignoring Him vanished in a moment's decision to return.

Jeannie stilled for a second, as he predicted she would. He caught her elbow and nodded, walking with her into a room where several members of Mike's family were busy with large pots, racks, lengths of string and stacks of cleaned honeycomb like the one Jeannie had just inspected. They were making the beeswax candles Richmond Farms sold in their gift shop.

Jeannie looked at Chad. He felt himself flush. "Birthday candles are an okay start," he offered, "but I think you're ready for an upgrade." She looked hesitant, but Chad tried to remember the surge of certainty he'd felt with he'd gotten—or God had given him—the idea. He was right about her readiness to move forward, he knew he was. She just needed a bit of coaxing.

She didn't reply, but she didn't turn to leave, either. Allowing himself the luxury of a hand on the small of her back, Chad led her up to the table where Mike had supplies for them set up.

She walked up to the table and touched the sheets of waffled beeswax that sat next to a pair of white string wicks, and a hot plate holding a tub of clear yellow liquid wax. When she turned to look up at him, his heart melted. "Just think of them as great big custom birthday candles," he encouraged, having trouble coming up with the right words. "You'll do fine."

"*You* will, too," she shot back. "I'm not doing this alone."

He hadn't counted on participating, but he couldn't very well back out now, could he? Jeannie jumped a bit when one of Mike's employees lit a large wick near where they were working, but she fought to regain composure. He wasn't good at it; his big hands made a fumbling job of rolling the beeswax around the wick when her candle was delicate and perfectly even. Her love of creating overcame her fear even faster than he'd planned. And beeswax was yellow—the whole room smelled of yellow sunshine and suited her perfectly. Before he could even finish one of his bumbling creations, Jeannie was on her third, experimenting with new techniques. He couldn't squelch the satisfaction he felt watching her delve into the process. Jeannie in the moonlight had stolen his kisses. He was pretty sure Jeannie by candlelight would steal his heart.

His eye caught a sign over the door of Mike's office: "Wisdom is like honey for you: If you find it, there is a future hope for you, and your hope will not be cut off. Proverbs 24:14"

Chad made the most startling discovery of the week: he still had hope. He fixed that new hope on one more project, the one he and Nick had discovered and would set into action later that week.

"Nicholas Nelworth, why are we heading to the river?"

"Because." Nicky kept tugging her toward the park along the riverbank.

She yanked her hand out of his grip. "Because *why?*"

Nicky groaned, finally giving in to her clear suspicion that "something was up." "Because this is where Chad and I have to go to do the thing we're going to do."

It was "Chad" now, was it? She crossed her hands over her chest. "It's chilly, and the riverbank concerts stopped three weeks ago. You're going to have to do better than 'the thing.' I'm not moving another step until you give me more to go on."

Nicky craned his head down past the walking bridge over the river, and Jeannie heard Plug bark a greeting in reply. "It has to happen outside. You need sky and a river."

He turned back to look at her. "I'm not supposed to tell you any more than that, so don't make me, okay? I don't want Chad to get mad."

The prospect of Chad and Nicky in cahoots was as unnerving as it was charming. Especially something with requirements like being outside at dusk near sky and water. "Okay, okay," she consented, letting Nicky pull her down toward the riverbank. The sun had fallen behind the hills, leaving twilight to wash the sky in amber and purple hues. She loved the river best at sunrise and sunset—the quiet grandeur of the water and the valley as the day began and ended could always soothe her soul.

Chad was waiting at the foot of the walking bridge, Plug beside him on a blanket. Next to him sat a box with oriental lettering. "You're not going to light off fireworks, are you?" The prospect panicked her. Chad wouldn't do that, would he?

Nicky laughed. "Nah, Mom, we wouldn't do that. But I thought that at first, too. It's different. You'll like it, I promise. Hey, there, Plug!"

At his call, Plug bounded off the blanket—actually bounded, something she'd never seen Plug do before—toward Nicky, nearly tackling him in a slobbery display of canine affection. Nicky's full-out laughter was pure joy to her heart, its rarity reminding her just how much they'd come through in the past few months. Chad's smile had the same effect. She sent thanks Heavenward. Perhaps they were finally walking out of the valley.

Nicky and Chad fussed over getting her settled on the blanket and setting the box between all three of them. Once situated, Nicky nodded at Chad, who cleared his throat the same way he had done before his fire safety presentation. She wasn't about to receive a lecture, was she?

Chad reached into the box and pulled out a pale disk of wood-ribbed paper, like a Chinese lantern. "There is a Chinese ceremony every spring involving lanterns like these." He handed the disk to Nicky, who knew exactly how to pop it open into a miniature paper balloon. "The Chinese use it to remember loved ones—" he cleared his throat again and she saw the muscles in his neck tense "—who have passed away. They send their hopes and prayers up into the sky in glowing lanterns."

Nicky fastened a little metal cage to the bottom of the lantern and handed it to her. "All of us have people to remember, so it's perfect. There's a little candle that goes in here, and the hot air makes it rise up into the sky, see?" He pulled a flat, round tealight candle out of the package and affixed it to its place in the cage.

"Like our birthday candles, only with prayers attached," Chad said, his eyes catching hers. "Laurie's mother sends these to me every year, but it was Nick who decided I ought to actually *use* them this year." She didn't need to ask who Laurie was; she knew by the shadow in his eyes. "Well," he added, wrestling back his composure as he handed another lantern to Nicky, "that we all should."

Jeannie caught her breath, stunned by how instantly and deeply the idea affected her. Lanterns, glowing and floating on the evening air—how beautiful it would be. And yet, it went so much deeper; it would be a lovely, poignant, painfully intimate moment for all of them. Maybe most especially for Chad. "You never lit the ones she sent before?"

"Couldn't manage it." His voice hitched

as he pulled out a third disc and began to pull it into the rounded shape. He and Nicky worked in silence for a moment, assembling theirs. Darkness settled in over the river, and Plug put his head on her thigh as if to say, "It'll be all right, just you wait and see."

Nicky lined the trio of lanterns up on the blanket, dropping the candles into the two remaining baskets. "All ready for launch. This is going to be so cool, Mom. I looked up photos on the internet." He sighed with satisfaction at the trio air fleet. "Dad would think this is awesome, wouldn't he?"

Nicky hadn't spoken of Henry since the fire. Jeannie could only nod, too full of feeling to attempt words.

"The lanterns had a second use." Chad extended a hand and pulled Jeannie to her feet. "When villagers had to hide in the mountains from their enemies, friends would light these and send them up to signal it was safe to come back home."

Safe to come back home. The words struck at the very heart of Jeannie's every longing. *Safe back home* seemed the dearest words in the world.

In careful quiet, they picked up their lanterns and walked to the river's edge. "Mine first," Nicky declared. He added, "Don't worry, I'll be careful," when Chad raised an eyebrow. "There's a fire extinguisher in the box, Mom, just in case you're wondering. Chad explained they'll burn themselves out and come down into the river after a few minutes." Clicking the long-necked lighter Chad handed him, Nicky carefully lit the tiny candle nestled inside the paper globe. "I christen you the S.S. Henry Nelworth."

Jeannie held her breath as the paper lantern began to glow like a flickering round moon. After a few seconds, Nicky gasped and said, "It's taking off, I can feel it!" He raised it up and slowly let it slide from his fingers. Like a silent prayer, it floated up into the night sky. She felt the release deep in her chest, saw it in Nicky's upturned face and heard it in the catch of Chad's breath.

It was all she could do not to break down as she lit her lantern and let it slip into the night. No christening or declarations were needed, just her hands reaching out into the darkness. She knew the moment held far more than the release of a simple lantern. Chad had given her something so deep she'd never know how to thank him.

Chapter Fifteen

Chad watched Nicky and Jeannie launch their lanterns, marveling at their faces as they did so. Amazing how something so simple could come to mean so much. Jeannie looked to him like a priceless, perfect gift, her upturned face and wet lashes watching the lantern glide from her hands.

Now it was his turn. It felt so much harder. He'd grasped his own lantern so fiercely that he'd actually pushed in a small dent on one side. Laurie would have laughed at that. He was sure he was shaking even though his hands were still. This felt so terribly important, so difficult, and yet so perfectly natural. Nick's ease paved the way, and Jeannie's wonder had pushed him on. He took a second step toward the river, selfishly needing more space between him and the world as he lifted the lantern. A split second of panic shot through him as he felt the lantern pull toward the sky, and he had to command his fingers to let loose.

When they did, he felt something slip free in his chest. Some hard shell finally cracked and fell away to let him take his first true deep breath in years. *It's safe to come home.* His prayer to Heaven and, he hoped, Heaven's message to him.

Jeannie sniffed behind him, and he turned to see her tearful eyes hold his gaze. Nick held her hand, the boy's own face flushed with emotion he was trying to hide. Chad held his hand out to her—to the both of them, really—and she walked forward to settle perfectly into the arc of his arm. Without a word, but with more than a few sniffles, they watched the trio of lights float farther and farther into the night sky. *Thank You, Lord. It's safe to come home.*

Plug, ever the clown, broke the mood by lunging to the edge of the water after an unsuspecting duck. "Whoa!" Nick yelled, setting off after Plug as he tried out his newly restored running skills down the riverbank.

"Don't go far," Chad ordered at the same

time Jeannie called "Don't wander off!" and they both laughed. In truth, he was grateful Plug had granted him some privacy with Jeannie. He had a lot to say to her, only none of it seemed to fit into words at the moment. He wished—prayed—to be the man he was years ago, the unscarred man who could easily let someone as amazing as Jeannie into his life. *All the way* into his life. "You lit that easily by yourself." The candles and lantern had done what he hoped—redeemed flame for her. It gave him the courage to hope he could heal enough to be the kind of man she really needed.

She grinned. "I did, didn't I?" Her smile dissolved into something more serious. "Thank you." Her glance flicked away for a moment, as if she were gathering the courage to say something. When her gaze returned, she licked her lips, took a big breath and asked, "Did you...let her go?"

She knew. And why wouldn't she? Hadn't she lost half of her own heart—her husband and the father of her son? What was it George said to him once, "Broken hearts recognize each other"? He was so deeply touched that she'd had the courage to ask, and so deeply disappointed that he didn't have the best answer. Still, he'd never lie to her; she deserved truth. "Some."

She pointed over his shoulder, and he turned to watch as the lanterns began to flicker. They were ethereal yellow balls in the sky, beautiful in how they danced close together, but each coming to the end of the candle that kept them aloft. She grabbed his hand as the first one went out. They stood silently as the other two surrendered to the night sky, gone to their sight and yet still there.

Chad turned back toward her, barely able to see her in the dim glow of the bridge light behind them. "I'm still here," she said softly, putting a hand up to his cheek. When she kissed him, his yearning to be near her won out over his last doubts. She was warmth to his ice, light to his dark, and he was so hungry to come out of the cold that he found himself wiling to pay any price to have that moment with her. He couldn't get near enough, couldn't hold her tight enough or long enough. He kissed her eyes, her cheeks, the back of her delicate hands, the exquisite curve of her jaw. He breathed her in like a drowning man's last gulp of air, terrified the moment couldn't last. Too lost in his need for her to care that it couldn't possibly last. Sure he would open his eyes and she would disappear into the night like the lanterns and leave him in the dark.

When he forced himself to open his eyes, when Plug's bark yanked him back to the real world, she was still there. She looked at him with brimming eyes, her face flushed. "Some is enough," she whispered as Nick's shouting came closer, her breath as ragged as his own.

"Stop fussing with my hair!" Nicky snatched the comb from Jeannie's hands. "Go fuss over Chad if you need something to do."

"Nicky!"

"Nick. Just Nick. Please, Mom, try?" Unsure how to handle Chad's deeper role in their lives. Nicky was prickly this morning. More than once he'd made some remark at breakfast about "Chad this" or "Chad that" falling into a teasing tone a younger boy would use about male-female relationships. While serious conversation became impossible, they hadn't fought, so Jeannie chose to view it as an improvement. He'd worn a burgundy shirt—the lightest color she'd seen

on him in a while, so she ignored the ever-
present dark, ripped jeans.

She spent a pleasant and productive pair
of hours finishing up some products in the
church kitchen, then drove home for lunch.
Chad's truck was outside the apartment when
she pulled up. He was waiting outside, a
large white envelope in his hands and a serious expression on his face.

"Did they deny my building permit?"
That was the building inspector's job—not
Chad's—but she couldn't think what else
would make him so stoic, especially after
last night.

"Nothing like that. Can I come inside for
a minute? We need to talk."

He was having regrets. She'd let him inside
her heart and he was going to pull away from
her. Blind panic, an illogical abandoned
feeling surged up out of nowhere. "What's
wrong?"

He took her hand, and she nearly sighed
with relief. He was still with her, he hadn't
retreated again—at least not yet. "I have
something important I want to show you.
Something I want you to think about."

"All right," Jeannie said unsteadily as she
turned the key in the door, sidetracked by

gratitude that she and Nicky had cleaned up the apartment when they got home last night. Hadn't Henry always said she cleaned when she was happy? She *was* happy—or at least she was until she saw the alarms going off in Chad's eyes. She knew, even before he spoke a word, even before he settled himself with disturbing seriousness at her kitchen table, that she wouldn't like what he had to say.

"Nick's a great kid," he started, his hands spread protectively over the envelope as if to hide its contents from her view. "A really great boy, but he's just that—a boy. A boy who's been through way too much. I'm hung up on the kid, really. Which is…why I'm here."

"What do you mean?"

"I want him to have a great life, to have every chance to succeed." Chad reached for her hand across the table. "Nick needs help, Jeannie. I wasn't certain until this morning, but I've had people up at the school watching for certain signs."

"You've been spying on Nicky? Without my permission?"

"Nothing like that. More like a heightened awareness for specific clues.

"You make it sound like you were hunting

for evidence. Chad, what is going on with you all of a sudden?"

Chad took a deep breath, keeping a hold of her hand. "Nick's been setting fires. Small things—garbage, sticks, nothing with any real intent to burn anything down—but it may not stay that way." She didn't like the authoritarian edge in his eyes.

"It was just some matches in his locker, Chad. He's acting out, yes, but you saw how much he's changed, even last night. We're almost over this."

"You said he went to a grief counselor when his dad died, and I know he's seen staff up at school since the fire…"

Jeannie felt her pulse thunder in her throat, pounding out any calm she had left "And he's doing *fine*. He's handling it. You said yourself that he'll come through this fine. Well, close to fine. Close enough."

Chad closed his eyes for a fraction of a second. "I care too much about Nick to let him go without the help he needs. I'm referring Nick to JFIP, the Juvenile Firesetter Intervention Program."

Jeannie yanked her hand away. "He's not some kind of criminal, Chad. You know that."

"Mrs. Hunnington told me his grades are far below what they were last year."

"He's been though a *fire,* for goodness' sake. *I* can barely concentrate. It hasn't even been three months, we're still living in boxes."

"He's been argumentative at school, and I know you said he's been more trouble at home."

"I think a teenage boy who's lost everything is entitled to a bout of bad moods, don't you?" She could feel her voice raising. He'd already done it, hadn't he? He wasn't here to ask her permission. "You've marked him for life, that's what you've done." She pointed at him, a sense of betrayal stabbing through her. "He cared about you, trusted you and you turned him in like some kind of deviant. How could you do that after last night?"

Chad shot up off the chair. "I haven't done anything yet, that's why I'm here. I'm here, now, *because* of last night, don't you see that? I care about him. I care about you." He turned and planted his hands on the table, towering over her. "He's in trouble, Jeannie. I tried to ignore the signs but they're all there. I can't pretend I don't see them anymore. Boys from single-parent homes are especially vulnerable…"

Jeannie stood up to him, fisting her hands because she wanted to hit Chad. "Don't you *dare* make this about Henry."

"I'm not!" Chad fired back, louder than she knew he wanted to. "He's set two small fires in back of the school. And Jeannie, listen to me. Nick didn't put the fires out. Kids who are just curious extinguish the fires once they set them but Scott told me Nick let them burn."

"Scott's lying, can't you see that?

"I can't prove that but I don't think he is. Nick's letting all that anger tangle him up inside and I can't stand there and watch him do something that really will mark him for the rest of his life." He paced the kitchen, running his hands through his hair. "Do you think I want to do this? Do you think for *one second* that I wasn't up all night wondering if it was the right thing to do? That I could be wrong? But worse yet, what if I'm not? He's at risk, Jeannie. Even if you can't see that, I have to. It's my job."

"I'm his mother. It's my job to know what's best for him."

"It's a two-day workshop. He'll get professional help and a completely confidential evaluation by a specialist. Would you rather take the chance he'll be arrested for arson some day? Take a life? Most kids who are like this get worse, do worse things than punch out some bully."

Jeannie stared at the envelope, feeling like the crisp black letters that spelled Davis County Fire Department Arson Prevention Program spelled out Nicky's doom. "My son is not an arsonist." Her words were as sharp and final as the letterhead.

"No, he's not. He's a mixed-up kid who doesn't know how to control the anger he feels. If he goes here—" Chad pointed to the envelope "—he'll get better ways to cope with all that. Look, the fire affected you—you couldn't bring yourself to light a match. Can you even allow for the possibility that the same events make him *need* to light one?"

"That makes no sense."

"Only if you won't look at it. This is a program specifically designed for kids like him. Run by people who know especially what he's facing. He won't get labeled by a two-day program."

Jeannie pulled the envelope toward her and dumped it out. "Won't get labeled? Do you really believe that?" She scanned the documents. "'For offenders ten to seventeen years of age.' Offenders. You don't call that a label?"

Chad's heart was shredding in his chest. *Offender* was an ugly word. His job was filled with ugly words. No, Nick wasn't an offender, but Chad's gut told him he was on his way. Chad hated what Jeannie's eyes did to him, hated how the betrayal cut through him, but he'd known it was coming. He'd decided sometime in the wee hours of this morning that he'd endure Jeannie's hate if it gave Nick a chance to pull back before things got worse. The phone call to school this morning had only confirmed what his instincts, his heart already knew. "He needs this." He hated how his surging emotions made his voice break, but he had to make her see that, even if she never forgave him for it.

"We trusted you." Tears filled her eyes. "He opened up to you, you said it yourself. He's already changing, already healing. And now you're going to turn him in?"

"I'm not turning him in, I'm getting him help. I can't get him there on my own. I won't shortchange him just because this hurts."

"What about last night? He could have burned those lanterns somehow, but he followed your directions. You handed him the lighter, Chad." The panic in her voice was killing him. She was trying desperately to deny it, frantic to hang on to her belief—to the *lie*—that everything was going to turn out fine for Nick if everyone just left him alone. "If you do this, people will think he was responsible for the house fire. Can't you see that?"

"No one at the department would think that."

"Maybe not at the department, but what about the rest of town? Once word gets out…"

"Word won't get out." Now who was believing the lie? She looked at him, and he couldn't really argue. She was right; he could do his best to draw the line between prevention and accusation, but precious few people would see it. He spent his entire job fighting the truth that prevention was essentially an invisible concept. "I'll be right beside you, both of you."

She pushed the envelope at him. "Oh, we've seen what happens to people who get close to you. No. I'm his mother and I say no.

Take this out of here before Nicky sees what you really think of him."

"Read it. That's all I'm asking."

"No."

"If you read it, and you don't recognize Nick in the descriptions, then…"

"It's not your decision."

The fact was a knife to his chest. It *wasn't* his decision. Without an actual criminal offense, he wasn't sure how far he could take things. He cared for her but couldn't control her. He'd lost his heart to her last night and it was too late to snatch it back. Now she was going to dangle his heart over a flame of risk so high he felt it burning already. She was going to break his heart all over again; it was only a matter of "when," not "if." Hadn't he known that? Hadn't he fought against all the vulnerable places he'd opened up last night, knowing it would only end in pain like this? He could refer all he wanted to, but he was essentially powerless if she withheld her consent. She could choose to do nothing and he couldn't stop it. Anger and panic and frustration wrapped around his throat like a noose. He couldn't find enough air to breathe.

"Just read it. *Please.*" *Dear God, You've*

got to let her see this. Save Nick. I'll swallow them hating me if You just save him.

"I don't know." Her words were sharp and clipped, and he realized he was too late. The look of betrayal in her eyes had already broken his heart.

Worse than that, it was clear he'd just broken hers.

Chapter Sixteen

"I hate it here." Nicky slammed the cabinet door shut when he got home after school. Jeannie closed her eyes and counted to ten. Any gains they'd made this morning were long gone in the bad day they'd clearly both had. He'd been a ball of anger since she picked him up after school, which only turned up the tension from her argument with Chad. The apartment seemed especially tiny this afternoon, stale and claustrophobic.

"I know things are hard right now," she said, trying to keep her voice calm and even, "but things are getting better, aren't they? We're getting through it the best we can."

"No. We're not. School's boring, home is gross, it all rots. I hate it here. My room smells funny and I need my other gym shoes and this bed is disgusting. It stinks, Mom. I'm sleeping on someone else's bed."

"I'm trying to get us to the new place as fast as I can." She couldn't even make herself believe it when she said it. "There aren't even real walls up yet above the store."

"Who needs walls?" Nicky moaned as he stomped toward his cramped room. It was just salt in the wound that he could barely fit himself and his backpack through the door at the same time. "Just get me outta here, Mom." *Slam.* His bedroom door shut with a cheap thud.

And Scott Collins's buddy shoved you into a locker today, but you're not going to tell me about that, are you? She'd suspected Nicky had kept from her the fact that episodes were still happening at school. It was getting harder to classify all this as just teenage backlash. Some things were better, but others were worse. Chad was helping Nicky cope, but too much was still going on at the school. There had been a phone message on her machine from the principal. When she returned the call to Mrs. Hunnington, she'd confirmed everything Chad said. She'd even added to things by mentioning the scuffle between Scott and Nicky. True to Chad's promise of confidentiality, she seemed to know nothing about the JFIP program. That did little to stop the spread of the cold knot of fear in her stomach.

Jeannie pulled a ham out of the freezer for supper, trying to ignore how the large white envelope seemed to yell at her from inside a drawer nearby. Scott belonged in that program, not Nicky. Nicky would be able to get his bearings if Scott would stop taunting him. She'd heard stories about parents who had to fight to get a bully recognized and dealt with, so it made her grateful Mrs. Hunnington and the rest of the school administration were acting, but they were acting against Nicky, too, weren't they?

"Still," the envelope seemed to jeer, "there's more." More than Scott Collins and his crowd of "junior thugs." Were they just exasperating what was already there, pulling Nicky's anger to the surface? One thing was alarmingly certain: Nicky was pulling away from her at the worst possible time.

He was, however, pulling toward Chad. It was good that Nicky was finally opening up to *someone*—and it stung that it wasn't her—but it would sting far more when Chad betrayed that precious relationship by throwing him into some drastic, criminal intervention program.

Jeannie wanted to raise her eyes Heavenward and yell, "Just get me outta here, Lord." *You love this boy,* Jeannie made herself pray instead. *You love him even more than I do. You made him before I made him. Teach me how to love him now. I don't know what to do with him.* Was it better he was lashing out, even if it was at her? Awful as it was to endure, was this at least healthier than keeping his anger bottled up inside? She'd endure a decade of this before letting him get labeled a deviant. *I'm at the end of my rope, Lord. I don't know what to do with Nicky. I don't know what to do with Chad. I don't know what's best for the store or even for me. I want to believe You do, but I can't see it right now.*

I can't see the path. The lament echoed in her head as she wandered around the kitchen, mindlessly wiping counters in an effort to put something of her life in order. *I can't see it.*

You won't see it. And he can. She stilled, frozen by the dreadful thought that Chad's relationship with Nicky might indeed let him see things she couldn't. Things she wouldn't.

Look at you, you won't even open the enve-
lope. Why is that?

Jeannie stood there, her hand on the
drawer handle, for what felt like forever.
Be the parent. Henry's words echoed in her
mind. Slowly, Jeannie pulled the drawer
open. Absurdly anxious that Nicky would
come storming out of his room at any
moment to accuse her of condemning him,
she ducked into her room with the packet and
shut the door.

Sitting on her bed—which felt, just as
Nicky had said, like someone else's old
bed—she eyed the envelope like the enemy
it was. She picked it up with two reluctant
fingers, gingerly, as if it contained beasts
waiting to devour her son.

Cold, clinical papers slid out, forms with
boxes and bullet points. At first, all she saw
were words like "offender" and "fire setter,"
ones she'd thrown in Chad's face. Worst were
the descriptions of things like "pyromania"
and "arsonist." That wasn't Nicky. Nicky
wasn't out to hurt people or cause harm; he
was just angry and provoked.

She read on, determined to disbelieve,
until she reached the page titled "Characteristics of Firestarters." Its contents stabbed

at her mother's heart, cruel and inescapably true. "Emotional release of displaced anger," and "heavy peer pressure" did indeed describe what she'd seen in Nicky. "Single parent families with absent fathers" hit her like a physical blow. Yes, there were things that weren't Nicky on these pages, but there were far too many things that *were* him.

It was as if the oxygen in the room were thinning out as she read, making her light-headed and panicked. Chad had been right; there were too many similarities in here to ignore. He may not need the full-blown program, but he needed the evaluation. She could no more wish this trouble away than she could wish away a broken arm. Some part of Nicky had broken, some deep part of him needed shoring up, support beyond just a mother's love. Or Chad's affections.

Tears of helplessness, of sharp-edged insufficiency, stole down her cheeks no matter how quickly she swiped them away. How sadly skilled she'd become at crying silently, sobbing in ways Nicky could not hear through the apartment's paper-thin walls. She felt Chad's broken-hearted lament of "I can't get him there on my own" burn into her own chest. Jeannie was just thinking how glad she was Nicky had turned his stereo way up—she was too wounded to care what the neighbors thought tonight—when the doorbell rang.

Abby pushed through the door with a pint of ice cream and her craft box. "Mary Hunnington asked me to check up on you two. I'll brought some of those new scrapbooking supplies I just got. We can make a page of Nicky's detention and expulsion letters. Blackmail for future girlfriends you don't like. Hey," she said, peering closer at Jeannie's eyes. "Whoa, you're not okay, are you?"

Usually, Jeannie welcomed Abby's kooky sense of humor. Her ability to laugh at the worst of events had pulled them through some dark times. There was no glossing over this. "No. We're not okay."

Abby deposited her things on the hall table and pulled Jeannie into a hug. "What's wrong? I mean what's wrong *now?*"

With one last check of Nick's shut door and blaring music, Jeannie motioned Abby into her bedroom. Once she shut the door behind them, Jeannie took a deep breath, feeling like she could barely form the words. "I need to...ask you something. And I need the absolute, unguarded truth from you."

Abby sat down on the bed, not even realizing she was right next to the condemning forms. "I promise."

Jeannie stood there, feeling bolted to the floor and ready to tumble over at the same time. The words came slowly, as if she were unearthing them from a deep, dark place. "Do you think Nicky needs…serious help?"

Abby's eyes began to fill with regret and tears. Jeannie felt herself spiraling down some dark tunnel, the same dark tunnel she'd tumbled down as Abby dragged her through the E.R. all those years ago. The same dark tunnel that started with the question, "Is Henry all right?" and hadn't quite ever ended yet.

"I think you've been unbelievably strong, Jeannie." Abby's sigh said the one word she hadn't spoken.

"That's a yes, isn't it?" Jeannie was crying now, clutching her borrowed bureau to stay upright.

Abby looked down. "That's a yes. He's not okay, Jeannie."

She couldn't hold the world up one moment longer. Jeannie sank down against the bureau and Abby flew off the bed to catch her in a fierce hug. "I want to go home," she wailed into Abby's shoulder, remembering how she'd wailed it in Abby's kitchen the night Henry died. She'd come to be so jealous of that kitchen. Abby's kitchen always hummed with love and smelled like sweet memories, and all she could think of right now was how much she hated the smell of this entire apartment. Even twelve of her new beeswax candles couldn't conquer the stale atmosphere—and oh, how the thought of those new candles hurt right now.

"Home's on its way." Abby rocked her like a child. "It's just not here yet." Abby's tears made her feel less alone. "Come to the house. Stay as many days as you need to."

Jeannie pulled herself up onto the bed, taking in a deep breath as she listened yet again for the volume of Nicky's music hiding her drama. "We both know that isn't a real solution." Maybe the real solution was in those horrid papers, but she wasn't quite ready to go that far yet. "No. We're stuck here. I just hadn't planned on hating it so much, you know?" Funny, the truth that she was stuck, the truth she'd avoided for so long, was surprisingly quiet when it came. Simple, peaceful almost. "And Nicky, well, he hates it even more."

Abby snagged a tissue box from the bedside table and plunked it between them as she sat down beside Jeannie. "I know. I know."

"I'd pitch a tent in the middle of Sweet Treats's studs and wires if the confounded occupancy permit could just come through."

"I know." After a moment of quiet, Abby picked up the papers on the JFIP program. "What is this?"

Jeannie summoned enough courage to give Abby a brief description of the prevention program. That, and a not-so-brief description of the fight she'd had with Chad over Nicky's need to participate.

"He has more courage than I do, and I'm your best friend."

"What do you mean?" She wasn't thinking of Chad in very heroic terms right now, even if that was a case of "shoot the messenger."

"Okay, cards on the table. I've been thinking Nicky was in hot water for weeks, but I wouldn't risk your reaction. Really, who wants to say that kind of thing to a mother? Me, I just kept praying you'd see whatever you needed to see in time. But Chad? He knew how you'd respond, and did it anyway. Because it was the right thing to do." Abby's voice got soft. "The right thing I was too chicken to do. How much must he care?"

"I hadn't thought about it like that. I think I was too busy being mad at him to realize this hurt him, too." Despite all the frustration, a part of her welcomed his protective—*over*protective—impulses. "I hate his suggestion and love him for it at the same time—is that possible?" Jeannie gulped, unprepared for the word *love* to slip out like that. Did he already mean that much to her?

"Do you love him?"

Jeannie pulled her knees up and hugged them. "It doesn't really seem possible in so short a time, does it?"

"You told me you fell in love with Henry on the first night. Why not now?"

"Last night, on the riverbank, I felt so much." Jeannie told Abby about the lanterns, whispering like schoolgirls sharing secrets. "When he kissed me, it was so strong it felt reckless. Unwise. Way too fast and furious for mature adults."

"Sounds like love to me."

"But so soon?" Jeannie shifted to face her dear friend. "Abby, it's like his faith is springing back to life right in front of my eyes. He fights to be close to me, I can feel it.

Up until today, he made me feel strong when too much in life makes me feel weak lately."

"Mom, can I have this ice cream?" Nicky voice came through the door, making Jeannie freeze and grab for the papers.

"Sure thing, kiddo," Abby called. "Take the whole thing." The two of them listened as Nicky rustled through the silverware drawer. "For a spoon, not a scoop," Abby whispered, and Jeannie felt the echo of a laugh bubble up inside her. "All of it straight out of the carton, I suspect." They heard Nicky's door slam shut and the music return to turn up again.

"Nicky thinks the world of Chad. This will kill him." Jeannie sighed, sure it would wound Nicky to have the man he so admired cart him off to some terrible program. Maybe there was no way around the initial pain. She thought of the way Chad had risked pain already, the way he'd laid his heart bare on the riverbank. That was the truest kind of courage, wasn't it? Yes, she could love this man.

Jeannie pulled herself up off the bed. "I need to make a phone call. You need to go home to Frank."

Abby gathered her into one last hug. "I

love you, and I want the best for you and Nicky. You know that."

"I do. Thank you for everything."

Chad answered on the first ring. He'd never been so glad to pick up the phone in all his life. He'd been staring at it, practically sitting on his hands to keep from dialing Jeannie, and now he didn't even wait for her to speak. "I'll be there in five minutes. Less."

He didn't know what the solution to their current situation was, he only knew he couldn't stand to leave things the way they were. He needed Jeannie. He absolutely couldn't abandon Nick to an easier path. He'd spent the past fifteen minutes praying fervently that God would show him the way out of this mess. Praying like he hadn't in years. He thought prayer would come back to him slowly, haltingly, but no. Once he started it was like eight years of floodgates unleashed and Chad found himself pouring his heart out to Heaven.

Jeannie grabbed his hand the moment she opened the door, but instead of pulling him into an embrace, she pulled him to the little area that served as a living room. "Explain to me," she said in a hushed voice, pointing toward the loud music coming from behind Nicky's door, "what will happen to my son if he goes into this program."

She'd read it. She'd read the listed characteristics of kids at risk and saw what he saw: that Nick was headed in a bad direction. How much pain was involved in a realization like that for a mother like her? That was Jeannie, finding her courage in the midst of so much pain. It only doubled the strength of his feelings for her. He challenged himself to spell out the highly detailed information in ways she could understand, keeping his thoughts clear and concise when his brain was racing in a dozen different directions. "Mostly, he'll meet with counselors who know this subject inside and out. And he'll talk with past teen offenders, kids who turned their behavior around."

"They'll watch him, won't they?" She chewed on a fingernail, and he noticed her makeup was all smudged. She'd been crying. He'd made her cry. Hadn't he told himself last night how surely he'd break her heart?

The music died down a bit from the hallway, and they both glanced back toward the bedroom door. He had to be careful here, but still he wouldn't deny her the truth. He took her hand and led her into the kitchen, farther away from Nick's earshot. "It's completely confidential, but I won't lie to you. If he goes through the program and still gets himself in a fire-setting situation, things will be… set in motion." Jeannie cringed, and Chad felt his heart twist. "But the success rate of JFIP is high. It works. He'll learn the consequences of fire-setting *before* he does it again. That's half the problem here—these kids don't think about the consequences. They don't get that others can be hurt, that permanent damage can be done."

She looked at him. "Our home and business burned. How can he *not* know fire does damage?"

"I think he does, somewhere inside. The anger is just tangling up how he thinks, confusing his impulses. Things boil up inside him until he can't keep a lid on it."

Jeannie leaned wearily against the counter, wrapping her arms around herself and closing her eyes. "I've prayed and prayed over him, over us, to keep us safe, to heal us and now this."

"I think," Chad said carefully, "this *is* the answer to that prayer. This is an *early* intervention program. I'm not signing him up to hang out with arsonists. He's going to be meeting with other kids who have his struggles. There's nobody at school or church who can really identify with what he's going through, Jeannie."

"We do. We've been through fire losses, both of us."

"We share his circumstance, but not his response. I meant what I said about your candles and his matches—fire's like grief. It hits people differently."

"But he's better for talking with you. Isn't that enough? Do we have to brand him 'at risk' like this?"

Chad took Jeannie by the shoulders. "Nick means the world to me, but I'm in over my head here. I can't stand by if there's something, *anything* out there that can do for him what I can't. I promise you, I'll be beside you every step of this, I'll watch over the process, make sure Nick gets every advantage."

"They'll know at school." They way she said it, he guessed she was imagining a file with "FIRESTARTER" scrawled across it in alarming red letters.

"Not necessarily. The staff doesn't know now, and they don't have to—although it's better if they do. As for the other kids, the programs are on successive Saturdays, two towns away, so none of his friends will know unless he tells them."

She eyed him. "You can't guarantee it won't get out."

Here was the painful truth. Confidentiality was a goal, a highly held ideal, but he couldn't guarantee no one would ever know. The janitor who'd found the ashes already had his suspicions. People talk. The small-town stereotype didn't come out of nowhere. "No, I can't. But I like that risk a lot more than I like risking he does something serious that we *can't* fix."

"He'll be angry."

"He's *already* angry, Jeannie."

"He'll hate me. And you."

"You're his mom. And I'm not going anywhere. We'll get through it."

He watched her fist her hands for the battle ahead. "I'll go get the papers. We'll tell him together."

"Nicky?" Jeannie knocked on his door. He didn't answer, but then his music was loud enough that he likely didn't hear it. "Nicky?" When another rap produced no response, she pushed open the door to an empty room. Nicky was nowhere in sight. The October breeze from the open window tufted out the olive-colored window curtains, giving her a full view of the fire escape, and the realization of what he'd done slammed into her.

She knew. She dashed to her bedroom where she knew what she would find— Chad's envelope, crumpled and empty. She had no idea how or why he'd gotten into her room without her noticing, but none of that mattered now. Why, *why* had she left that envelope out on the bureau?

Chad was quickly behind her, his worried glance flicking back and forth between her and the envelope. "He saw these. Chad, he saw these and now he's gone." Funny how she'd thought that access to the fire escape would give Nicky an extra measure of comfort. What a tumble of mistakes she'd made at the worst possible time.

Chad backtracked. "He can't have left, we'd have heard him." She followed his steps down the hall to Nicky's room, only to hear him moan when he saw the open window. "Oh, no."

Jeannie rushed to the window, peering out into the courtyard. It was empty, save for a crumpled piece of paper rolling to the corner, blown by the wind. There was no doubting now: Nicky had seen the papers and run.

When she turned, hands on her pounding heart, Chad was in full emergency response mode. Calm, clear and determined. "He can't have gone far. He's not in any danger."

"You know what he's thinking. I thought it. He's running, Chad. He's scared and I don't know what he'll do. You said it yourself. He's barely able to control himself and all that anger, and I've just made it ten times worse."

"He's upset, yes, but I don't think he'll hurt himself or anyone."

Jeannie doubled back into her room to fumble through her purse and speed-dialed Nicky's phone. From Nicky's bedroom, she heard the cell phone ring, telling her he'd left it behind. He didn't want to hear from her. When she made it back into the room, Chad had dumped Nicky's backpack out onto the bedroom floor, revealing the still-ringing phone and two more lighters. Chad took her hand. "Let's figure out where he might have gone. Can you call Abby's or a few friends' houses where he might be? If you want, I'll scout around the building and up the block."

"Yes, go. I'll get on the phone."

Abby had no help to give. "Oh, Jeannie, no. Not now, not with those papers!" She and Abby divided up friends to call as Jeannie tried not to give into worry. How could he have gotten so far so fast?

Fear had gripped her the first time she saw those papers. How could it be any different for Nicky? They were wordy documents, filled with psychological terms, but even Nicky would know what words like "arsonist" and "offender" implied. "Nicky!" she called at the window, praying he'd answer, "Nicky, we need to talk. It's not what you're thinking!" Another five minutes of searching produced nothing but mounting fear as the daylight faded. Her cell phone rang and Chad's number came on screen. "Is his bike around?" he asked without greeting. "He can't have gone far if he's on foot."

Jeannie checked and found the bike gone. "Chad, his bike is gone. That means he could be anywhere by now. It's getting dark."

"Or it could mean he's riding around blowing off steam. Try not to jump to conclusions, okay? Does Nick have keys to the shop?"

It took her a moment to get her brain to

work. "Yes, I gave him a key to the back door padlock last week."

"I'm just around the corner. Give your shop keys to me and I'll send George over to wait if he shows up there."

She fumbled to pull the key from her ring while she waited for Chad. Was Nicky reading those frightening descriptions right now, thinking that's how people saw him? Would he do something drastic if he jumped to any of the wrong conclusions? Who knew what a frightened, angry thirteen-year-old could do?

"Keep that panic at bay, Jeannie." Chad was beside her, wrapping his hands around hers as she handed him the keys. "He'll be okay," he said, piercing her fog of worry with his gaze. "We'll find him, we'll get him to understand. He'll be okay." He took her face in his hands, and she felt his calm feed hers. His quick kiss had a sense of strength, as if he were breathing courage into her.

"Try school and any other place you can think of. I'll start at the river and go north." He glanced at his watch. "It's seven-thirty. I'll check in with you in twenty minutes no matter what, but we'll call if either one of us hears or finds anything."

Chapter Seventeen

He regretted leaving her. If it weren't the fastest way to find Nick, he'd never have left her side. He was planning to be the one to tell Nick about the program, hoping Nick would take any anger out on him rather than put his mother through more strife.

Don't let anything happen to him, Lord. His affection for Nick was tangled up—in the best of ways—with the powerful things he felt for Jeannie. He'd never saw himself as the "dad" type, but his thoughts traveled to what it would be like to go to Nick's baseball games, to take him fishing, maybe buy him a dog of his own. *Find him,* hummed in his lungs with every breath, until the gut-level desire became a continual prayer: *Let me find him, help me find him, show me where he is, keep him safe until I get there.*

Gravel spun under his tires as Chad pulled up beside the riverbank. It was getting darker, which wasn't helping things at all.

"Nick!" he called, hearing his voice echo off the water. "Talk to me, Nick." The boy was smart, it could get tricky if he didn't want to be found. In half an hour the full dark would only make it harder to find him.

Ten minutes of searching proved fruitless. A pass around the riverbank in the dwindling daylight, and then another with a flashlight, produced nothing but an old newspaper and one discarded sneaker. Chad's heart sank as he checked his watch, realizing he'd reached the check-in time empty-handed. *Let her have found him,* he groaned as he flipped open his phone and dialed Jeannie.

"Did you find him?" Her voice was tight, which told him instantly she'd had no results, either.

"No." The word stuck in his throat. "But it will be okay. He'll come home, or we'll find him." He said the words as much to himself as to Jeannie. He wanted to believe his God-given instinct would lead him to Nick.

"He has to be somewhere nearby. Look for a bike, a red bike with black stripes." She was losing her fight to stay calm, he could hear it in her voice.

"Hang on, Jeannie. He'll be okay. He's just being clueless, running on emotion and not even thinking what this is doing to you. I'm going to hang up now so I can keep looking. You do the same. And…"

"And what?" Her voice was so thin.

"And try to remember God's still watching over Nick. Even now."

"I'll try," she said, sniffling, "but it's hard."

The small click of his phone shutting echoed through the darkness of the riverbank where once he'd basked in Jeannie's glow. He stood for a moment in frustration. *Find him. Help me find him.* Nothing. Chad heard nothing except the sound of his own teeth grinding. His gut told him Nick was here. Kids set fires in important places. He knew this place was important to Nick. *He wants to be found,* Chad prayed as he swept his flashlight again around the long, narrow park. *Even if he doesn't realize it. Come on, God. Cut that boy a break.* Chad cupped his hands and yelled, "Nick! Nick, I'm sure you're here and your mom is worried. Whatever it is it can't be so bad we you and I can't figure it out, okay?"

Something glimmered in his flashlight beam. The spoke of a bicycle tire. Then a red fender with black stripes.

Off to his left, a burst of orange flames shot up off a rock by the water. A boy's yelp, then a splash as the flames surged high and fast. Burning paper.

"Nick!" Chad broke into a run, finding Nick standing knee-deep in the river watching a small pile of leaves and white papers burn on a flat rock. Without even thinking, Chad nudged the boy aside and bent down to push his arms into the water, forcing a wave to wash up over the rock and douse the flame.

They stood there for a moment, puffing and wet, both too shocked to say anything. "Are you okay?" Chad finally pulled out of his stunned silence to grab Nick by the shoulders. "What on earth were you doing?"

"Proving you right!" Nick shouted, scrambling out of the water. "Go away."

"I need to talk to you about what's on those papers."

"I don't want to talk to you. You just think I belong in jail."

Chad followed him up the bank. "I don't. I think you need help."

"Oh, great, you, too. Why won't everyone just leave me alone?"

"Because we care about you."

"Oh, yeah, I hear that all the time. You care enough to ship me off to jail. I'm not dumb, I read what's in those papers. You think I set my house on fire, just like Scott. The school assigned you to watch me, didn't they?"

"Is that what you think?" Chad sat down on the riverbank, hoping it would induce Nick to do the same.

"You're sending me off to some fire program."

"I know for a fact you didn't start the fire at your house, Nick, and I can prove it."

Nick just looked at him with narrowed eyes. Chad could see behind the anger, however, to a scared little boy who just wanted to know he wasn't going to jail. "Nick, sit down."

He paced for a moment, fidgety and resistant. Chad waited. Half of him wanted to pull out the phone and let Jeannie know, but another half of him recognized the need stay in the moment. "I knew you thought you did, so I went back and checked the records. It wasn't you."

"I know that." Nick sat down.

"A surge in the wiring system started the fire. Anything could have set the spark—a toaster, a hair dryer, anything. Anything but *you*." Sure, Nick had a host of other problems, but Chad was sure most of them stemmed from the need to hear this particular truth. Right now, when it counted most. "You didn't do it, Nick. Listen to me. It's not your fault. Things just happen sometimes. They're bad things, and we're part of them, but it doesn't make us guilty." His own words struck him. Chad realized he wasn't just talking to Nick; he was talking to himself. About Laurie's fire. The realization made him love the boy all the more. "I had something bad happen to me and I made a whole lot of mistakes because of it, so I get how this feels. I get how you're all mixed up. It doesn't make *us* bad. We're just in pain, and people in pain don't always *think*." He pointed to the smoldering pile of wet ashes on the rocks.

"It felt good to set them on fire. It was stupid—I know that—but I wanted to burn them away. I make the fire do what I want. I can make it start, I can make it stop." He waited a long, raw moment before asking, "Is that why you're sending me to jail?"

He would have pulled the boy into a tight hug right there and then. "No. You aren't going to jail. I'd like it, though, if you'd let some people help you with what's going on. Inside, I mean. With the matches and the lighters and why that urge hits you the way it does." Chad sighed, feeling like the two of them had climbed out of some black pit and could now rest at its edge. "You've had so much happen to you, I just want to do everything I can to make sure you come out of it okay. These people know how to do that."

"I don't want to go."

"I know it looks hard, and scary." Chad could no longer help himself and put his arm around the boy, who shivered under his grasp and then finally leaned against him. "I promise you, Nick, I'll be right there the whole time." The moment was so real, so unbelievably deep, that Chad's chest physically hurt. *An actual heartache,* he thought oddly to himself. *Or maybe just healing hurts more than I thought.*

"Mom, too, right?"

"Absolutely." The promise was as much to Jeannie as to Nick. "Speaking of your mom..."

"She's pretty mad, isn't she?"

"She'll be too relieved to be mad."

Nick looked up at him. "What bunch of mistakes did *you* make?"

Explain eight years of guilt and regret to a thirteen-year-old? Is there a simple way to tell him about years of self-imposed exile? Foolish distance? Chad realized, with a sense of truth that struck hard, that he'd run off, too. He'd just done it on the inside. Maybe he'd sensed that in Nick all along, and that's what drew him so inexplicably to the boy. "I thought I should have been able to stop Laurie from dying in that fire." The words nearly caught in his throat. "But I realize now that I couldn't have. I did lots of dumb things because I didn't realize that before."

"So we're sort of the same, huh?"

Nick's sheepish smile cut through the last of Chad's reserve, and he pulled the boy into a fierce hug. "Yeah, we're the same in lots of ways. I think that's a good thing."

"It's not so bad. Only…"

Chad pulled back to look at the boy. Already Nick's face had changed completely, the tension replaced by what he hoped was affection. "Only what?"

"Only I think Mom will be a whole lot madder at me than she will be at you."

Chad laughed, relief flooding his chest. "If I wait any longer to get you over to her, I doubt that will be true." He rose and extended his hand to pull Nick to his feet. "Let's get going, okay?"

Nick shook the leaves off his jacket. "Yep. I'm wet, anyways."

"I'm really glad I was the one to find you." Chad pulled the phone from his pocket as they walked up over to Nick's bike, preparing to deliver the best news possible to Jeannie.

He was flipping it open when Nick reached out and stopped him. "She likes you, so you think you could put in a good word for me? You know, so maybe I'm not grounded for the rest of my life or anything?"

"Now you're way out of my jurisdiction, kid. I've got no pull..." Chad stopped short as the wail of the firehouse alarm filled the night. He and Nick looked at each other, their thoughts both going in the same direction: Jeannie.

Looking and waiting was making Jeannie crazy. Everything that could be done was being done, and it still wasn't enough. The sheer inactivity of driving around town looking for Nicky was torture. *Lord, I can't think of what else to do. You've got to help me think of what else to do,* she prayed. She'd fought so hard to keep Nicky from sliding under the blackness of grief and loss. She'd dug her heels in, determined to muscle him through all the tragedies that his young life had endured, and it hadn't worked.

"I can't sit here and do nothing!" she said aloud, banging at the steering wheel with her hands. "*You* can't let him go through this awful mess and sit there doing nothing."

Her panic, yelled so nakedly to God, shocked her into remembering Who and what she believed. When had she lost the rock-hard truth that all things still fell under God's sovereign hand? Maybe Nick *needed* to go through this awful mess. In her endless shouts at God tonight, had she ever prayed for God to do whatever He needed to do *in Nicky's soul* tonight? Or in hers or Chad's?

The fire had burned her trust, robbed her of the strength to say "Thy will be done." That trust had been what had held her up during her grief. During the slow climb back into life, that kind of trust would have let her see Nicky needed help long before Chad had to force the realization on her. She'd substituted that trust with a scurrying, solution-grasping frenzy.

God was trustworthy and always had been. Even tonight. All the time working. He'd never once pulled His gaze from her. He knew where Nicky was at this very moment and knew what would happen next.

That new peace was shattered by the worst possible interruption: the fire siren. *No, it can't be. He can't have gone and set something on fire.*

Chapter Eighteen

Jeannie slammed on the brakes and dialed Chad with shaking fingers. "Chad!" It was a yelp of pure fear.

"I've got him!" Chad's voice burst through the crackling connection. "He's here and he's fine and I've got him."

"Oh, Lord, thank You!" Gratitude melted the tension of the past hour. Jeannie couldn't decide whether to scream or cry. "Just what did he think he was doing?"

"Mom...." Evidently she'd shouted it loud enough for Nicky to hear. Even at a whine, the sound of his voice was the sweetest thing she'd ever heard.

"He just wasn't thinking," she heard Chad say.

"The sirens..."

"It's not him, but I haven't reached George on the phone so I don't know what it is."

"Is he okay?" Concern still warred with anger, with no clear winner as yet.

"Yes," Chad answered, "and I don't think he'll pull a stunt like that again anytime soon."

"I'm *fine,* Mom," Nicky chimed in and she could almost laugh with the relief of hearing his voice.

"And what *else* are you, Nick?" Chad cued her son.

Nicky's voice replied from a distance. "I'm...sorry."

He sounded so small and reluctant, Jeannie could nearly cry for the bliss of knowing it was over. How clearly she could imagine them driving toward her, together. What a wonderful picture they made in her head. "You'd better be," she said. "Don't you ever, ever do something like that again, you hear me?"

"Where are you?"

Jeannie had to take a moment and look around, having lost track of where she was. "At school. On the corner by the baseball fields."

"I'll meet you at Sweet Treats. We should

be there in five minutes. I'll tell George and you can call Abby. Drive safely now, okay? The engines might still be coming out of the bay and you're all wound up. The last thing we nccd is an accident."

The man of constant protection. While it had chafed at her before, right now it was a comfort. The smile on her face grew wider—something she hadn't thought possible. After a jubilant call to Abby she put the Jeep in gear and made her way down to Tyler Street. Still a crazy pendulum, her emotions swung between not being able to concoct a sufficiently painful punishment and wanting to never let Nicky leave her sight again.

She was closer than Chad, and pulled up to the shop to see a flurry of activity in the firehouse. A second set of engines was prepping to leave. They weren't huge red monsters anymore. They were her friends and neighbors, her fellow citizens and…and the man she loved. All of them working together to keep Gordon Falls safe. All she could feel as she stared at the trucks was deep gratitude.

Chad's pickup pulled up and the two of them piled out of the cab. Nicky looked older, darker somehow. He was slumped inside his jacket, head down, hands stuffed in his pockets. When he looked up, the shadows melted off his face to reveal the frightened, sorry baby boy of years gone by. Chad had somehow gotten through to him. She ran toward him in a flurry of need.

He stiffened in her hug at first, the way boys his age do, but it was only moments before he softened against her. She pulled back to inspect him, running her hands into his mussed hair, wiping away a smudge on his cheek, scowling at his wet jeans. He rolled his eyes, but they glistened, too. "Are you all right?"

"I'm fine."

She gave his head a little shake. "Why? Why, Nicholas?"

"It just sort of burst out of me. I saw those papers and I just...exploded."

"He'll go to the fire-starters program," Chad said. Jeannie held his gaze. Something had changed in him, too. Did it have something to do with Nicky? She saw a look flick between them, and realized God had indeed been in all that happened tonight. Chad's eyes held a soft surety, the final barrier between them torn down. "He did set those papers on fire down the by riverbank, but that's not the reason for the siren."

"You *what?*" Jeannie caught Chad's eye over Nicky's head.

"I doubt it will happen again," Chad replied. "We're on the right track now. All of us."

"Thank you," she said, feeling like the words didn't come close to what needed to be said. She peeled one hand off of Nicky to extend it toward Chad, and he took it with none of his earlier hesitation. His hand encompassed hers with a new strength, his eyes fired with even more warmth than she'd seen before. "I'm so glad you were the one to find him."

He swallowed, and she could see his throat work to keep his emotions in check. "Me, too." It barely came out above a whisper.

"I would have come home after a while," Nicky added, evidently needing to keep Chad's heroics in their proper perspective.

"Well, you'll be home a good long time, mister. You're grounded until I can come up with something worse." Nicky looked like he saw that coming, offering no more resistance than a gulp and a shrug of his shoulders. The sheer mention of home reminded her just how tired she was. Suddenly every part of her body ached, her neck and shoulders seemed to be nothing but knots. "I think it's time we all go home and put ourselves back together." She wiped a bit of grime from Nicky's chin. "You go wait in the car. I've got to talk to Mr. Owens for a moment."

Evidently Nicky hadn't lost all of his attitude in the chaos. "Oh, I'm *sure* you do," he said with a theatrical disdain as he turned toward the car.

Jeannie caught his elbow. "But not before you thank Mr. Owens for what he did tonight."

Nicky turned back and dragged his gaze up to Chad. "Um, thanks. For everything." It wasn't nearly as reluctant as Jeannie expected. Something really had transpired between those two tonight. She wondered if she'd get it out of Nicky, or if she'd need to wait and talk to Chad. As it was, Chad stared at her as if he had a lot to say but knew now wasn't the time.

"I won't keep your mom long. Don't ever make me do that again." Chad gently cuffed the boy. "I'm too old for this sort of thing, and you're too smart."

Chad's hand found hers and clung to it as

they watched Nicky climb into the Jeep. Her throat tightened up as she turned to Chad. The desire to find out why he looked so different—and to tell him how she felt about him—warred inside her with the need to be beside her son. Nicky had been the center of her universe for so long, it felt odd—not wrong, just odd—to have someone else vie for her heart's focus.

Chad's thumb ran tenderly along the back of her palm. "You need to go be with Nick, and I'd better go over there." He nodded toward the firehouse. "But I need to talk to you. Soon. I...well, there's a lot to say."

Jeannie squeezed his hand. "Come by when you're done?"

"It might be late."

She'd wait. She needed to unscramble the day with him beside her. She needed to know why his eyes held such a different light, what had finally gotten through to Nicky, needed Chad to know her heart. "I'll be there."

"Okay then." He hesitated for a split second, then leaned down and planted a quick, careful kiss on her cheek.

Jeannie could not leave it at that. She flung her arms around him and kissed him. This time there was no resistance, no tension, as if the tight binding she'd always felt in him had been cut loose. She felt his cheek come down to rest on the top of her head, felt his arms clasp her tightly. "Thank you, " she said again, not bothering to squelch the small sob that came at the end of her words. "Thank you for finding him."

The Jeep's horn beeped, and Chad pulled back to look at her, swallowing hard. "We sort of found each other. I'll tell you later, I promise. You go home and I'll be there soon enough."

He loved her.

Chad walked across the street in a stunned silence. He'd been in love with Jeannie maybe for weeks now, but wouldn't allow himself to admit it. He'd managed to convince himself she couldn't possibly feel the same way about someone like him, but that unsinkable sunshine spirit of hers kept pushing through his defenses. Her affections, the light of her amazing spirit kept seeping into cracks and thawing frozen places until he had no choice but to love her. He'd tried to turn away, tried to deny what he felt, what she made him feel. He'd blocked her at every turn without even realizing it. He'd blocked

God's every attempt to reenter his life, too, until Jeannie had helped to push that door open again as well. To a faith of his own, not the echo of someone else's. What a gift Jeannie Nelworth was. What a fool he'd been to push that gift away for so long in the name of "mourning."

Somehow, life had gone beyond "mourning Laurie" into some sort of "refusing to live" that Laurie would never have wanted. How sad she would have been to watch guilt strangle Chad's faith like this. *I've gone so very wrong, Lord. I've done no honor to Laurie's memory. Grant me the chance to start over, here, with them. I'm begging You.*

"Structure fire by the old graveyard," George said as Chad pushed open the firehouse doors. "I could use you."

"Sure." For the first time in years he'd climbed into his gear with only adrenaline raising his pulse, not the tight twist of irrational fear that had choked him before.

Someone had doused a gardener's shack by the historical cemetery with gasoline. A disturbing prank, the kind every firefighter dreads will turn into something worse. "These kids never think it will get out of hand," a fireman had said as they held a hose to the tiny building. "If I get my hands on the hooligan who started this..."

It isn't Nick, Chad told himself as they worked to contain the blaze. *It won't be Nick. Not now. We got him in time.*

Chad went back to the firehouse and shed his gear, feeling weary enough to sleep a week. He was aching to see Jeannie, to hold her, but another ache demanded one more thing of him. So, despite the hour, Chad pulled his truck beside the historic cemetery that now lay wet and glistening in the moonlight.

He made his way through the soaked grass to a small, rounded marker that looked like the one marking where Laurie's ashes had been strewn. He rarely went to that place—it was a hundred miles away and Laurie was rejoicing and free in Heaven to him, not marked by marble. If he went anywhere, it was to the three trees he'd donated in her name to the local arboretum. They were the best earthly tribute to her.

He somehow knew this was farewell. The goodbye to her needed to be tonight, and he was sure Laurie would be okay with right here. Maybe she was even telling him "here, now," for the thumping in his brain sounded so much like her low, musical voice.

The marker was cold and coarse, but he put his hand to it anyway. "I loved you," he whispered, the words heavy with exhaustion and the torment of the past eight years. "I love her." He'd loved Laurie, but dying with her wasn't what God wanted. Life allowed second chances—for him, for Jeannie, for Nick. Jeannie would never cancel out the place Laurie had held in his life; Jeannie was the healing balm to the wounds of guilt he'd inflicted on himself. Wounds God had seen fit to heal as He pulled Chad back toward Himself.

Chad looked up at the moon—the moon that had looked down so kindly on his first kiss with Jeannie—and felt the chaff of eight wasted years blow off him in the night wind. Life was starting over tonight. The turning point for all of them had finally come. There was only one place to be, only one woman to be with, only one thing that needed saying.

"Nicky told me everything," Jeannie blurted out the moment Chad was inside her door, mostly because she needed to say it and she was worried that if she gave in to the urge to fall into Chad's arms, she'd never speak again. "He really thought people accused him of our fire? I thought he knew better than to believe something like that from Scott Collins. No boy should shoulder that kind of pain. Not even for a minute."

"As for Scott Collins, George just phoned. It was Scott Collins who set tonight's fire. George recognized his dad's initials on the bottom of the gas can we found by the shed. Scott confessed when George went over there after the fire."

"Scott set the fire."

"It explains why he'd been egging Nick on, and a lot of other things. Nick will go the prevention program, but Scott now has actual arson charges against him."

"Arson charges. Oh, Chad, that could have been Nick. We need to get him into that program. How could I have denied he needed this when...?"

Chad shushed her. "You are his mother. You see the boy you love, not the part you can't fix. Guilt...guilt makes us go blind." The finger he'd placed on her lips feathered down her cheek, making Jeannie's head spin. There was no hint of the shadows that so often came across his eyes, only a rich deepness of peaceful green. "I know a thing or two about it. I think…I *know* God put you and Nick in my life because of it."

"Thank you, Chad." She leaned against him. "For what you are to Nicky…*Nick*." She looked up into his eyes, not in the least bit afraid to say what she felt. "For what you are to me."

"You're amazing, you know that?" He touched a lock of her hair, his eyes falling shut for just a moment at the contact. For a second she thought the floor swayed under her feet. There was no restraint in him, but also no tension. He was grimy, exhausted, but totally at peace. "Did you know I woke up this morning thinking about the way your hair feels? I'm not used to such gushy stuff." He let his arms slide around Jeannie, and she melted into the perfect circle of his embrace. "Talking to Nick tonight, well, it opened up my eyes. I hadn't realized how much guilt I still carried or that it had built up such a thick wall. I'm ready to get back to life. To faith. To you."

He used to stumble on words about faith before, now he spoke with clarity. To see such weight lifted from him told her she'd underestimated the depth of his pain.

"I'm so thankful God gave Nicky someone who understood his struggle." She wanted to burst out that she loved him, but she knew he needed to be the first to say it. Instead, she sighed and slid her hands to his chest. His heart was thumping wildly under her hand—as wildly as her own pulse pounded.

He pulled her closer, his gaze making her knees buckle, his breath dancing over her neck and his hands wandering across her back. "Thank you," he said, letting his forehead fall against hers. "I'm in love with every brave, polka-dotted bit of you, you must know that by now."

Jeannie's smile filled her whole body. She left small kisses on his cheek, thinking he smelled of smoke and courage. "I suspected the feeling was mutual. Your quiet is ten times braver than my busy, do you know that? I love that about you. I love you."

Chad pulled back with solemn eyes. "I want a life that includes you and Nick. I can't imagine a life that doesn't include the two of you. You want that, too, don't you?"

"With all my heart." She kissed him. After all the jolts of the evening, it was like waking up slowly to a welcome truth. The kiss quickly ignited into a tumble of pent-up hope that left them bumping against the wall like teenagers on a front porch. It was joyful, the healing opposite of every dark fear the night had held, until the latch on Nicky's door clicked open and they froze.

"Oh, man," Nicky groaned as he swiped his hair out of his eyes, "I was afraid it was you two." There wasn't a hint of surprise in his voice. In fact, he seemed a bit annoyed at the whole thing.

"Listen, Nicky.... Nick..." Jeannie was absolutely stumped for what to say. Surely she'd kissed Chad before, but she was suddenly torn between dropping Chad's hand and hanging on to it for dear life.

Nicky leaned against the opposite wall and rolled his eyes. "Puh-lease. You've been all googly-eyed since Aunt Abby's. It's not like I'm five or anything."

Jeannie felt Chad's hand tighten on hers. "So you're okay with this?" he asked carefully.

Nicky looked at Jeannie instead, narrowing his eyes. "Will I get grounded less time if I say yes?"

"Absolutely not!" Jeannie replied, then pulled out of Chad's grip to give her son a hug. "But say yes, anyway."

"I'm fine." He extricated himself from Jeannie's hug. "Actually, I'm hungry. Do we have any more popcorn?"

Epilogue

February 2010

Chad had never been more nervous in his life. He watched in agony as that "thing" the Gordon Falls Merchants Association claimed was a key made its way up the block. No one could ever remember how the Gordon Falls business opening tradition had gotten its start, but for years now a large decorated key would be passed up the street from merchant to merchant until it reached the new business owner to signify its official opening. This week, the week before Valentine's Day, all of Gordon Falls was anticipating the reopening of Sweet Treats. Especially him. He'd thanked God every day that Jeannie and Nick had come through the holidays better, stronger and healing. Nick was doing well after the JFIP program, his grades back up and the boy's brighter nature returned. They'd moved into their new home two weeks ago, and the world was falling peacefully into place.

Except for today. Today, Chad was on the verge of panic. Only Abby and Nick knew why.

Chad groaned as the "key" came closer. Abby's taste for excess had run its course; the key was a shocking bubble-gum pink hue and coated with rhinestones. Even worse, a too-big polka-dotted yellow bow fluttered in the chilly February breeze like garish kite tails. He felt in his pocket for the addition he would make to that key, tried to stay calm and keep his breathing easy. This was a delicate operation, a crucial moment. *Don't blow it. Stay calm.* Chad gulped as Principal Hunnington plunked the heavy key into his hand.

Abby, according to their plan, threw up a handful of yellow confetti to make a diversionary fuss. Chad twisted out of eyesight and fiddled with the key for the ten seconds Abby's distraction provided. He doubled the knot in the bow, took a deep breath and passed the key on to Pastor Allen. The minister grinned when he saw the addition, but said nothing as he passed it to Nick. With a sheepish thumbs-up to Chad, Nick passed the key to his mother.

A cheer went up as Jeannie took the key, did a silly little jig and flipped the sign on Sweet Treats's front door to OPEN. For a heart-stopping moment, Chad couldn't see her through the crowd now pressing up against the entrance. Then, as a highly female sound pierced the air, Abby managed to part the crowd between them so that he had a clear view of Jeannie. She held up the ribbon tied to the end of the key, dangling the diamond ring he'd tied to the polka-dotted fabric.

Jeannie came at him like the ball of sunshine she was, hitting him at full speed with an embrace that took his breath away. It was as if all the joy in the world exploded right in front of him, as if the length of his life lined up to this moment. He could barely make out her "Yes!" from the flurry of kisses she planted everywhere. Laughing and catching her up in a spin of bliss that felt too good to be true, Chad let himself be carried away by a wave of cheers as those around him caught on to what had just happened. Even Plug howled in approval.

* * * * *

Dear Reader,

No one likes pain. Even if it is the most effective way to create change, it's hardly the most pleasant. God can always redeem the worst pain, even when we can't see how. We get into trouble when we hoard our pain for ourselves rather than give it to the Great Healer. Chad learns he's held on to his pain far too long; it has choked his life surely as the smoke he fights in fires. Jeannie has spent so much of her energy focusing on the sweetness of life that she's denied her pain and Nick's. All three of them need God's touch, and I delighted in crafting the story of how they all brought each other closer to His healing and restoration. I hope their sweet story gives you hope for whatever pain you are in, and that the love they find helps you see the love waiting in your own life. As always, I love to hear from you at www.alliepleiter.com or P.O. Box 7026, Villa Park, IL 60181.

Questions for Discussion

1. Have you ever tried to smile through a big problem, pretending it's all okay when it isn't? What works about that strategy? When does it go wrong?

2. Do you think George's dog-walking scheme is brilliant or misguided?

3. Would you have scheduled the fire drill for Nicky's school? Why or why not?

4. Sometimes animals really do help us heal—has this happened to you? What did they give you that a human friend could not?

5. When has a silly-but-real fear derailed you like Jeannie's fear of lighting a match? How did, or didn't you get over it?

6. Do you think Abby is meddling, or nudging her friend out of a "stuck" place?

7. How did you handle the last time a family member made a huge mistake like

Nicky's expulsion? What would you do differently?

8. Nicky says "nobody gets what it's like" to survive a fire. What's happened in your life that people have a hard time understanding? What can you do about it?

9. Do you agree or disagree with Chad's idea that his faith was weak because it started out as admiration of Laurie's faith?

10. What food gives you "the caramel swoon"?

11. Do you have a friend with the most wonderful gift of showing up when needed? Have you thanked them lately?

12. What do you think of the Chinese lanterns? Would you welcome something like that or find it pretentious?

13. Presented with the scary concept of the fire-starter's program, what would you do in Jeannie's shoes?

14. Jeannie realizes Chad can see part of

Nicky she can't. When has a friend served that role for you?

15. Chad says that bad things happen "and we're part of them, but it doesn't make us guilty." Is that true for you or not?

LARGER-PRINT BOOKS!

**GET 2 FREE
LARGER-PRINT NOVELS
PLUS 2 FREE
MYSTERY GIFTS**

Love Inspired

Larger-print novels are now available...

YES! Please send me 2 FREE LARGER-PRINT Love Inspired® novels and my 2 FREE mystery gifts (gifts are worth about $10). After receiving them, if I don't wish to receive any more books, I can return the shipping statement marked "cancel". If I don't cancel, I will receive 6 brand-new novels every month and be billed just $4.99 per book in the U.S. or $5.49 per book in Canada. That's a saving of at least 23% off the cover price. It's quite a bargain! Shipping and handling is just 50¢ per book in the U.S. and 75¢ per book in Canada.* I understand that accepting the 2 free books and gifts places me under no obligation to buy anything. I can always return a shipment and cancel at any time. Even if I never buy another book, the two free books and gifts are mine to keep forever.

122/322 IDN FEG3

Name _____ (PLEASE PRINT) _____

Address _____ Apt. # _____

City _____ State/Prov. _____ Zip/Postal Code _____

Signature (if under 18, a parent or guardian must sign) _____

Mail to the Reader Service:
IN U.S.A.: P.O. Box 1867, Buffalo, NY 14240-1867
IN CANADA: P.O. Box 609, Fort Erie, Ontario L2A 5X3

Not valid to current subscribers to Love Inspired Larger-Print books.

**Are you a current subscriber to Love Inspired books
and want to receive the larger-print edition?
Call 1-800-873-8635 or visit www.ReaderService.com.**

* Terms and prices subject to change without notice. Prices do not include applicable taxes. Sales tax applicable in N.Y. Canadian residents will be charged applicable taxes. Offer not valid in Quebec. This offer is limited to one order per household. All orders subject to credit approval. Credit or debit balances in a customer's account(s) may be offset by any other outstanding balance owed by or to the customer. Please allow 4 to 6 weeks for delivery. Offer available while quantities last.

LILP11B

Love Inspired SUSPENSE

RIVETING INSPIRATIONAL ROMANCE

Watch for our series of edge-
of-your-seat suspense novels.
These contemporary tales
of intrigue and romance
feature Christian characters
facing challenges to their faith...
and their lives!

AVAILABLE IN REGULAR
& LARGER-PRINT FORMATS

For exciting stories that reflect traditional values,
visit:
www.ReaderService.com